C. Y. Barlow

Helen MacGregor

Or, conquest and sacrifice

C. Y. Barlow

Helen MacGregor
Or, conquest and sacrifice

ISBN/EAN: 9783337015909

Printed in Europe, USA, Canada, Australia, Japan

Cover: Foto ©Raphael Reischuk / pixelio.de

More available books at **www.hansebooks.com**

Old Dugald, the blind harper.   p. 14.

HELEN MACGREGOR;

OR,

CONQUEST AND SACRIFICE.

BY
MRS. C. Y. BARLOW.

———◄•••►———

PHILADELPHIA:
J. C. GARRIGUES & CO.,
No. 608 ARCH STREET.
1869.

WESTCOTT & THOMSON,
Stereotypers,
PHILADELPHIA.

Jas. B. Rodgers, Pr
52 & 54 N. 6th St.

CONTENTS.

3

VI.

VII.

VIII.

IX.

X.

XI.

XII.

XIII.

XIV.

XV.

XVI.

XVII.

XVIII.

XIX.

1 *

XX.

XXI.

XXII.

XXIII.

XXIV.

HELEN MacGREGOR.

I.

THE HIGHLAND HOME.

"All twinkling with the dew-drop's sheen
    The brier-rose fell in streamers green,
    And creeping shrubs, of thousand dyes,
    Waved in the west wind's summer sighs.
    Boon nature scattered free and wild
    Each plant or flower, the mountain's child."

SUNLIGHT, the glorious sunlight of a summer
morning in the Highlands of Scotland, was
glinting with its early splendor the mountain tops,
but had not yet reached the dark moor, the loch, nor
the deep vale of the Scraggan Glen. On the edge
of the wild moor stood a solitary cottage, or rather
hut, built of turf. Everything around it looked
neglected, and it lacked that air of neatness which
usually distinguishes the Scottish farm house.

7

There was some attempt at a rude garden, which had been won from the waste around, but the enclosure was broken, and a small Highland cow was walking through it, and making herself perfectly at home by eating whatever took her fancy. A rough bench, on which were some fishing-rods, stood outside of the door, and some dozen dogs lay in different directions, within a few yards of the hut.

This poor dwelling, with its squalid poverty, contrasted ill with the beauty of the scene around it. Through the sweet freshness of the early morning the eye looked to the dark back-ground of the mountains, clothed to the very summits with the sturdy oak and lofty pine, near whose gnarled roots

> " The primrose pale, and violet flower,
>   Found in each cliff a narrow bower;"

to the moor, covered with the wild heath flower, on whose every bell hung the dew tears of morn waiting the warm kiss of the sun; to the loch in its calm beauty; to the little cataract, "that laugh of the mountain," with its noisy babble; while the ear drank in the thrilling notes of the forest songsters. It was a lovely spot, such as a hermit might choose, to "look through nature up to nature's God."

The door of the hut opened, and a young girl came out. Bounding with light step to where the little mountain stream made its last jump for the valley, she stooped and bathed her face in the stone basin which caught its waters. Then dipping in her long dark hair, she sat down on the grass, and soon twisted it into curls, which she bound with a scarlet ribbon. This scarlet snood was Helen's only ornament, and she prized it highly. Her father returning once from a distant parish had, in an unusual fit of liberality, bought it for her. She immediately threw away the old faded blue, and, notwithstanding Margaret's scolding, continued to wear it altogether, laughingly declaring that when that was gone her father would buy her another. Her simple toilet finished, Helen sank back in the heather, unmindful of dew, and gave herself up to the enjoyment of the hour. Passionately she loved all nature, true mountain child that she was. The bird, the bee, and the flower were her sole playmates, and many an hour of precious time did Helen lose in vague dreaming.

The sun peeped into the Scraggan Glen, and lighted up the old hut into a sort of wild beauty, but all unmindful of his burning presence, the girl still reclined, with her elbow on the ground, and her head on her hand.

"Helen! Helen!" called a sharp voice, and a little wrinkled old woman, dressed in a blue skirt and short gown, came out of the hut, and shading her eyes from the sun with her hand, looked round for the missing child.

Helen rose slowly, and walked leisurely towards her. "What is it, Margie? Here I am."

"What is it, Margie? Did any one ever see such a daft bairn? Is there nothing to do, do ye think, of a wash day, but to be learning a sang of the cuckoo, or laying ye're thriftless length in the heather? Ye don't earn your salt."

"And why should I earn my salt?" asked Helen, with a gay laugh. "Now, Margaret, have not you told me, hundreds of times, that I was the daughter of a MacGregor, and that the MacGregors were born ladies and gentlemen? And now you ask me to work! I'm astonished at you, Margaret!"

Fun danced in Helen's eyes, as with a very long

face she made this speech, and then turned to play with the dogs.

This saucy reply, so far from vexing the old woman, seemed to afford her an immense amount of pleasure. She went into the hut, chuckling to herself, and repeating, "Oh, she's the canny one, she has the real old bluid, the real old bluid," and the thoughts thus occasioned made her old face smile for the next half hour, as memory recalled the days of her youth, when a bright Scotch lassie, she had waited on Helen's grandmother, and carried Helen's mother in her arms, in the grand days of the MacGregors. And so it happened now, that the saucier Helen was, and the more authority she assumed, the better it pleased the faithful old servant, who fondly saw in it a remnant of the ancient aristocratic spirit, showing itself in the midst of poverty. She was used to her young mistress's moods. It did not therefore surprise her when, upon coming out with the tubs, she saw Helen unfasten her gay plaid, and merrily help to carry the clothes down to the loch. Margaret hated new styles and customs, and thought whatever was oldest was always best. Therefore putting some clothes in a tub, and pouring fresh water

on them from the loch, she motioned to Helen
who with a merry laugh jumped in, and commenced treading the clothes with her bare feet.
She danced about, and splashed the water in her
very face, and not a little fell to Margaret's share,
who was industriously tramping in another tub.
But the higher the water splashed, the louder
rang Helen's clear laugh, till old Ben None caught
up the echo, and repeated the rippling notes, far
off among the hills.

But old Margaret, who the better pleased she
was, the more she grumbled, muttered crossly,

"Ye're as crazy as a loon."

"Ah, well, Margie, no loon to-day is as happy
as Helen MacGregor."

"Happy!" exclaimed the old woman, treading
more vigorously, "little happiness contents ye, if
ye find it here."

"A little!" said the girl, throwing off the water
from her dark hair, while the drops hung like
tears from her eyelashes, and deepened the crimson
on her cheek. "A little! why, what Highland
lassie climbs our mountains with as free a step as
I? I can find the brightest heather bells, and the
deadliest night-shade, and each streamlet's greenest

water-cresses. I know the witches' cave, and the haunted hollow, where the fairies sing. Happy!" she continued, with a gay laugh, "why I'm happy treading these clothes, happy when I wait on surly brother Malcom, happy here, now, and everywhere. Oh, the world is full of pleasure!"

Margaret looked at her curiously, and half envious of the youth and joy she saw in that glowing face, she said, "Ah, weel, weel, ye always was a strange bairn. Hand out the clothes. Ye're born, but ye're ne'er buried, and there's mony a lang path with no light to it."

"No matter, Margie, I'm not the lassie to beckon a sorrow that may never come."

"It will come. It will come," was the reply. "I've seen the ruined hearth-stone, once the hame of the MacGregor, on which rests the stranger's foot. I've heard the Banshee wail for the last chieftain, and I see the lone hut in the Scraggan Glen, where my poor bairn is growing up like the wild roe of the mountain, untaught, unloved. Ah, woe to the ending!"

"Margaret, it is enough," answered Helen, and the tears for a moment moistened her eyes, "when sorrow really comes, the daughter of the Gael must

2

learn to bind her plaid o'er a broken heart, with-out a murmur."

She stood a moment in thought, then shaking her head, she recommenced in a gay tone, "but, Margaret, why will you recall the past, and sigh over the uncertain future? You cast the gloam-ing over the beauty of this sunshine. You tire me. You vex me. I will not be sad. Good luck ever attends the brave and loving, and no wicked fairy shall have the power to mar the bright future of a true daughter of Scotland's mountains. See yonder on the rocks is old blind Dugald, the min-strel. Good-bye, then; I seek more cheerful com-pany."

And Helen, wrapping her plaid around her once more, sprang lightly up the rocky pathway.

No word had passed her lips, of faith in the over-ruling providence of God. None, of his gra-cious promises to those in trouble or affliction. Good and bad luck, and good and bad influences and omens, were the only religion in which Helen believed. Her father never went to the kirk, nor ever troubled himself about his soul's salvation, and as the nearest parish was some miles distant, and Helen had never been taught to go, she staid away also. Thus in a country abounding in gospel privileges, Helen was growing up as wild, untutored, and careless, as her own mountain flowers. The superstitious tales of an old woman, mixed with her own wild fancies, were her chief mental food. True, the minister did leave his comfortable manse, and walk the bleak moor as often as possible to the solitary cottage, for the good of its inmates, but he seldom saw Helen, for she was nearly always away on some wild expedition of her own, and the reception he met with from Donald MacGregor, was such, that he was loath to repeat his unwelcome visit. So Helen drank in the beauty and life around her, without one grateful thought of the bountiful Giver.

"Good morning, Dugald," she said, seating herself beside him, "I have come to hear the saddest, weirdest song ye know."

The old man touched the harp that lay beside him, and brought forth a few sad notes, then stopping suddenly, he asked,

"What shadow rests on the mountain's pride to-day, that her voice is sad?"

"Margaret has been scolding and worrying."

The old man shook his head, and with a smile

replied, " Well does Dugald Stuart know, that when Margaret scolds, Helen laughs. But it is wrong to cast the saddened visions of age over the bright dreams of youth. Who expects yonder tiny cataract, babbling and leaping in the morning sunlight, to rest calm and placid as the loch, sleeping in the deep shadow of the mountain?"

Helen was indolently reclining on the rock, waiting for the song, but seeing the old man lost in a reverie, after his last words, she sat up, and taking the harp, struck a few notes, and then in a clear, ringing voice, commenced singing an ancient war-song.

The old man, roused from his musing by her wild song, listened with pleased attention. Helen, with her love for music, her sweet voice, and her buoyant spirits, had won her way years ago to the old minstrel's heart. He was a lonely man. Afflicted from childhood with blindness, he made a scanty living by wandering about, playing on his harp. Helen never had anything to give, yet Dugald had taught her to play almost as well as he could; and the remembrance of Helen's merry laugh, and joyful welcome, often turned his footsteps towards the Scraggan Glen, where indeed he was treated as an honored guest; for Helen ever longed to hear his sweet music, and heroic songs, and Margaret was ready to lend an ear to any gossip that might be afloat in the distant parishes.

As Helen sang, another listener was added to her audience. Emerging from behind a projecting rock, some distance above, a gentleman seated himself, and looked down upon the scene below. He had an artist's eye for the picturesque, and the sight which burst upon his view charmed him into silence. The beautiful loch, bordered by blooming heather, the old hut looking red and warm in the sunlight, the still dark glen stretching far away, sleeping in the shadows of the majestic trees—on the rock below him the old man with his head thrown back in a listening attitude, and his white hair streaming in the wind, the young girl by his side, her plaid thrown carelessly on one shoulder, her hand resting on the harp, her eyes sparkling with enthusiasm, and her beaming face answering to the joy-notes of her musical soul,—all joined to form a picture that would have attracted even an indifferent observer. The song again commenced. This time it was a coronach, or ancient Highland dirge, on the death of a chieftain.

2 *   B

CORONACH.

"He is gone on the mountain,
　He is lost to the forest,
Like a summer-dried fountain,
　When our need was the sorest.
The font, reappearing,
　From the rain-drops shall borrow,
But to us comes no cheering,
　To Duncan no morrow!

"The hand of the reaper
　Takes the ears that are hoary,
But the voice of the weeper
　Wails manhood in glory.
The autumn winds rushing
　Waft the leaves that are searest,
But our flower was in flushing,
　When blighting was nearest.

"Fleet foot on the correi,
　Sage counsel in cumber,
Red hand in the foray,
　How sound is thy slumber!
Like the dew on the mountain,
　Like the foam on the river,
Like the bubble on the fountain,
　Thou art gone, and forever!"

The song ended with wild thrilling sweetness, and the stranger came down the narrow pathway, and advanced to where they were sitting. Dugald instantly touched Helen's hand, saying,—

"A strange step, my lassie," and turned his sightless eye-balls towards the stranger.

Helen glanced hastily up, and judging the gentleman from his dress to be a clergyman, she rose and courtesied. The clergyman, for such he really was, after wishing them good morning, sat down on the rock, and entered into conversation, with the ease of a polished gentleman. There was something in the pleasant tones of his voice, that won the ear of the blind minstrel, and he soon found himself in an earnest dissertation on ancient poetry and song. Helen had been brought up in too free and careless a manner to dread the presence of a stranger; indeed she rather hailed his arrival with delight, as a pleasant variety to the monotony of her existence. Besides, Helen, with the quick instinct of a child, noticed that all his conversation bespoke a deep reverence for religion, which she admired but had never been taught to imitate. And there was something in the bright blue eye, and kindly smile, which would have won a confidence harder to gain than Helen's. As it was she sang for him song after song, and listened with pleased attention to his instructive discourse.

Thus the sun reached the mark of high noon,

ere the group on the rock were aware of it, and Margaret's shrill tones were heard, summoning Helen and Dugald to dinner.

The stranger, having walked many miles in the bracing mountain air, was not loath to accept Helen's cordial invitation to share their noon-day meal. So he followed the light springy step of the girl down the steep mountain path, with a little more caution, but with equal readiness.

II.

THE LOAN.

"The sounds of thy streams in my spirit I bear—
  Farewell! and a blessing be with thee, green land!
 On thy hearths, on thy halls, on thy pure mountain air,
  On the chords of the harp, and the minstrel's free hand!"

AS the clergyman entered the hut, preceded by Dugald and Helen, he took in at a rapid glance the scene before him. The small room was furnished in the simplest manner. A few wooden chairs were to be seen, and a wooden table. On one side was a rude kind of closet without a door, and in the closet stood a few rough dishes; opposite to that the wall was ornamented with the antlers of a huge deer, supporting a long fowling-piece. The table was spread with a snowy cloth, and Margaret was bending over the fire, taking up some fish, which emitted a very savory odor. In one corner sat a tall, dark man, whose haughty features showed too plainly the ravages of time, and

21

of uncontrolled passions. Towards him Helen advanced, saying,

"My father! a stranger waits."

Donald MacGregor instantly rose, and the clergyman was not a little astonished at the stately politeness with which he was received. He judged at once, that the man before him had not always lived in that rude style. He saw with sorrow the traces sin had left on that otherwise noble face; and he felt that, if affliction had fallen to his lot, it had not been met with the submissive spirit of the Christian, but had been repelled by his native pride, as an unjust punishment, and had fallen as a fatal shadow over the life before him.

And all this was too true. Donald MacGregor, born to an ancient patrimony, and a high name, had been cheated of the former by the dishonesty of a relative, whom he loved as a brother; and from that day, with a cynical indifference, he buried in obscurity the name and the talents, of which he had once been so proud. He came to live in this lonely cottage, in the wild Scraggan Glen, followed by the faithful Margaret, who would never forsake the children, Malcom and Helen, whose mother had been dead several years.

Here, in this solitary spot, Donald gave himself up to idleness and bitter musings. Day after day he studied revenge, and cherished rebellious thoughts. The relative who had wronged him was a clergyman, and at once, with the sweeping accusation of the headstrong, he denounced all religion as foolishness, and all ministers as hypocrites; forgetting, as some writer remarks, that one of the greatest proofs of the worth of religion, is that rogues are anxious to wear its livery, the better to conceal their purposes, well knowing that the name of Christian places its possessor above suspicion.

The stranger introduced himself as the Rev. Clement Ashton; and it required all of Donald's politeness to enable him to give a welcome, to answer the demands of Highland hospitality. But whatever his feelings were, there was nothing in his behaviour to indicate that his guest was not to his liking.

The simple meal was ready. It consisted of a plate of fish, a dish of potatoes, some oaten cakes, and a pitcher of milk. But, ere it was partaken of, Mr. Ashton, with a slight bow towards his host, raised his hand, and asked the blessing of God upon the meal before them. He well knew, from the conversation he had held with Helen, that the Lord was unhonored, and His name an unwelcome sound in that household; but Mr. Ashton had learned the command of His Divine Master, to let his light shine before men. Aye, the deeper the darkness, the more need, he felt, there was for the redeeming light of the Sun of Righteousness. So ignoring the fact that Donald would not talk upon religious subjects, he skillfully turned each topic towards the one great duty of life, which always silenced MacGregor until that subject was exhausted and a new one was introduced.

Donald was heartily glad when the dinner was over, and making a graceful apology to his guest, took his gun from the wall, and disappeared. Old Dugald, the minstrel, went next. Margaret commenced clearing the table, and Mr. Ashton proposed that Helen should accompany him part of the way on his homeward track. She joyfully assented. Wandering over mount and moor was her chief delight. Mr. Ashton had asked for this walk, that he might talk to the young girl of the dear Saviour. He never expected to see her again, and he longed even in that brief time to speak a few words, that might, through God's grace, make a lasting impression.

They had wandered on for some time in silence, Mr. Ashton drinking in the beauty of the scene around him, and pondering how best to open the subject; while Helen ran lightly from one object to another. At length they came to a wild hollow, densely shaded by birch and oak, in which twilight still lingered, although it was high noon. Mr. Ashton gazed at the dewy freshness and wild beauty of the dell, as it contrasted with the glare of sunshine above, and was about proposing to Helen that they should descend into it, when the girl stopped, and seating herself in the shadow of a tree, said smilingly,

"I can go no further. Yonder dell is the home of the shaggy men; you must not cross it; your path lies up this steep mountain; the way is long."

"Why should I not go through the dell?" asked the clergyman, "I see no men there."

Helen gave a gay laugh, as she answered, "You may lock long ere you see them, but they are ever there. Dinna ye ken that brownies and fairies are hard to see? You can win the shaggy men by

3

kindness sometimes, but ye must not enter their homes."

"Ah," said Mr. Ashton, "you have nothing to fear from such folks."

"Fear!" said the girl, contemptuously, "I am a daughter of the Gael; I never fear. Besides, the canny people ne'er yet hurt a harmless lassie."

"You misunderstood me. I meant there was nothing to fear from such people, because they do not exist; there are no brownies and shaggy men."

Helen opened to their widest extent her great brown eyes, and looked at him in amazement. Brought up, and taught what little she knew, by the ignorant and superstitious old Highland woman, Margaret, at the tenderest age she had been frightened into obedience by the positive assurance, that one of the shaggy men was even then outside the door waiting to take her. When she was a little older, Margie took delight in showing her all the dark mysterious passages and caves around her wild home, and in filling her childish mind with legends and superstitions, living now only in the memories of the old. Helen's mind was clear and sharp beyond her years. Her imagination loved to revel in the ideal and beautiful, as well as the

fantastic and grotesque.   Some of these marvellous
tales she neglected, as too improbable.   But those
she liked best she retained, to add a kind of frightful charm to her lonely walks.   And she so peo-
pled the mountains around her with the bright
creations of her own fancy, tinged by Margaret's
superstitious tales, that she sometimes really imag-
ined she saw forms deep in some dark cave or cleft
in the rock, and then starting away, she would
reach home so breathless and excited, that she
would be greeted by Margie's exclamation, "Did
ye see the Banshee?" meaning an old woman in
a long blue mantle, who, she believed, appeared to
foretell the death of some distinguished person.
But Helen, naturally courageous, would never admit that she had been frightened; and indeed this
seldom occurred.   She had learned to love these
fairy imaginings, and to feel a tender interest in
these children of her fancy.   She never plucked a
flower from the fairy grotto, although the flowers
there were most beautiful.   She trod with the
lightest, and most careful step over their dancing
ground, until she persuaded herself, as they must
know all this, that they must have learned to love
her.   Indeed these fairy spirits, and her father's

dogs, were Helen's sole companions. No wonder then that she looked astonished at any one doubting the existence of creatures that seemed living realities to her. She dropped her eyes, and shook her head, with a bright smile at Mr. Ashton's remark, as much as to say, "How foolish you are!"

The clergyman waited a while, then asked,—

"Have you ever seen any of these little shaggy men?"

"Oh, yes, often."

It was now Mr. Ashton's turn to smile. Helen looked up and caught the expression.

"Well, well, you do not believe it. Come here at the gloaming, and sit on yonder rock until night has clothed the mountain, and you will doubt no more."

Mr. Ashton did not answer at once. He was thinking how he could best convince the child that she was wrong. He felt that merely contradicting her would do no good. He glanced thoughtfully at the animated face and speaking eyes, and sighed to think, "She knows nothing of the lovely Redeemer: nothing of the bright home he has gone to prepare. How my Miriam would love this girl, and instruct her. What would she say, if I should bring her back with me, a daughter?"

Helen looked, and wondered at his silence, but presently she ventured to interrupt it.

"Will you try it, sir?"

"Will you come with me?" he asked.

"Ah, that would break the charm; you must bide alone. And I would not come, in any case; he who gets the ill will of the fairies, has sair luck."

"The entrance of Thy words giveth light." This text floated through Mr. Ashton's mind. "Yes," he thought, "I will tell her the simple story of the cross. I will try to lead her young mind to believe in the all-sufficient power of that God, who alone holds the universe, and measures out the evil and the good."

He commenced with the garden of Eden, the happiness and the fall witnessed amid its blooming shades. He told the perfect life of the Redeemer, the full pardon through his shed blood, and the glorious hope held out for all. Helen listened eagerly. To her it was but another fairy tale, more wonderful, more touching and beautiful than the legends of her own wild land, but still

3 *

only a story after all. Then, with simple earnestness, he tried to make her feel, that that Saviour
died for her; that she must be washed in that par-
doning blood ere she could go to dwell in heaven.
Helen was deeply touched; tears stood in her dark
eyes; and Mr. Ashton lifted up his heart in a silent prayer, that the seed might fall into good
ground. How different would his feelings have
been, could he have looked into Helen's thoughts.
She was thinking how good and kind it was of
the Saviour to die for sinners, to save those
who had done wrong; but the idea that *she* was a
sinner, she would have rejected with haughty
scorn.

And as her eye glanced up to the sky, and
rested on the dark cloud hiding the summit of
the mountain, no thought came into her mind,
that over her soul hung the dark cloud of self-
righteousness and pride.

Mr. Ashton noticed the clouds gathering above
them, and rising hastily, said he must be going.

But just at that moment, Donald MacGregor
appeared, with his gun on his shoulder, and some
heath-cock which he had brought down for supper. Much as he disliked his guest, he knew too

well the danger of sending any one out, when a storm was brewing in the mountains. He therefore begged the clergyman to return with them to the hut.

Mr. Ashton had no inclination to be caught in the rain, and the thunder was already beginning to mutter; so they all returned with rapid footsteps to the cottage, and had just reached it, when the storm burst.

What is like a storm in the mountains? So sudden, so grand, so terrible. It swept around the little hut, in its fierceness, as though it would carry the rude structure away.

Another person had been added to the group who were listening around the peat fire to the storm—Helen's brother Malcom, a youth of about nineteen. He was a shepherd, and kept the sheep of a wealthy farmer some miles distant. He went early in the morning, and remained all day; and the longer he staid away, the better it pleased Helen, for he well deserved the nick-name she gave him, "Surly Malcom." He took special delight in ordering Helen around, and in obliging her to wait on him, and then never troubled himself to thank her, while her father sat by unheeding

and unreproving. Mr. Ashton was not a little
astonished at the readiness and good humour with
which she obeyed. But now and then her cheek
would flush, and an angry light dart from her
eye; and he thought, with sorrow, that a life led
under such trying circumstances, with no religious
training to counterbalance the evil, would soon
spoil all Helen's good qualities. Before the evening was over, he felt strongly interested in the
young girl. He felt that, with proper Christian
training, she would make a noble woman, and he
took a sudden resolve, one of those impulses which
honor the warm hearts from which they spring.

Helen had left the room for a few minutes, and
he turned to MacGregor and said,

"Does Helen attend school?"

"She does not," was the short and haughty answer.

Mr. Ashton then went on to speak of education,
of its importance to the possessor, of its powerful
influence on the world. Clement Ashton was an
eloquent speaker. Donald MacGregor was an
educated man. He listened at first in silence, but
soon yielded himself to the charm of refined conversation, to which he had so long been a stranger.

His prejudices were forgotten for the evening, as the hours passed swiftly by; and when, before retiring, Mr. Ashton asked permission to have worship, he gave a ready consent. Upon seeing the Bible brought up, Malcom, who had sat in sullen silence most of the evening, rose and left the room.

Mr. Ashton read the twelfth chapter of Hebrews, which teaches so plainly how we should receive the chastening rod. Then followed an earnest prayer for the spiritual welfare of that family.

When they rose from their knees, all felt solemn. Never had MacGregor felt so deeply before how he was wasting his precious hours; how days were following days, and no good deeds, no noble actions, were being registered by the recording angel in the book of life. Remorse stirred to its very depths the heart of the proud man, as he looked on his only daughter. How was he training her for life's duties, and for the solemn hour of death? Mr. Ashton could not have spoken at a more favorable time.

As Helen, with a graceful good night, left the room, he said,

"You have a lovely daughter, sir."

c

"Yes," he answered slowly, "she grows like our heath-flowers, as beautiful, and as wild."

"I am a stranger to you," said the clergyman, "excuse me, if I seem presumptuous. We were just speaking of education, and you acknowledged its value; then why not educate Helen?"

"I was not aware, sir, that you had any special interest in my family," answered Donald, haughtily.

"Pardon me," said Mr. Ashton, hastily, "if I have taken a strong interest in your daughter. I have no children, and my heart has been strangely touched for this girl, brought up in this bleak home. Lend her to me a while,"—

MacGregor's brow darkened, and an angry reply rose to his lips, but Mr. Ashton hastened to add:

"Do not be offended. I know it is a great favor to ask, and it takes you by surprise. My wife would cherish her fondly, as her own daughter. Oh, sir, how can you answer at the last day, for denying to your child the knowledge of a saving faith in Christ Jesus? Let her have a few years of Christian culture, and she shall return to you, God willing, to be the light and comfort of your home.

"I am a stranger to you; come to Edinburgh, if you wish for recommendations,"—

Donald interrupted him hastily, "I wish none. 'One gentleman is quick to recognize another.' When I trust at all, I trust fully. You shall know to-morrow."

What thoughts were with the neglectful father through the silent watches of that night? Did the ghosts of former years stand round him, showing him the long array of misspent hours, and slighted duties?

Or did God's Holy Spirit strive yet once more, to waken him to a higher life?

He had ever been more proud of his daughter, than fond of her. He acknowledged to himself in spite of his skepticism, that Mr. Ashton was a true Christian; and looking forward to the years yet before him, he could see no other way of disposing of Helen. As to letting her go out to service, as many another Scotch lassie did, it was out of the question. To that his pride would never consent.

And it was perhaps, after all, this very pride that won his consent. Helen would be educated, and brought up like a lady, in a manner fitting her birth; and if she did imbibe the religious faith of her tutor, it would do her no harm.

Thus a parent's pride was sending Helen to a distant home; and no fond parent's prayer went forth in her behalf, to plead before the great white throne, that the eternal Eye of mercy might look on all her childish errors, and the eternal Arm protect her in every danger and temptation, for the sake of the crucified One.

The next morning Helen MacGregor was loaned to a stranger, with the promise that she should return in five years.

Five years! Life, death, eternal bliss, or eternal woe, may be wrapped in that brief space.

Five years! the Omniscient Eye alone can read their mystic record.

III.

"To thee the love of woman hath gone down;
Dark flow thy tides o'er manhood's noble head,
O'er youth's bright locks, and beauty's flowery crown;
  Yet must thou hear a voice—Restore the dead!
Earth shall reclaim her precious things from thee!—
  Restore the dead, thou sea!"

BUT how did Helen like this change in her destiny? To a girl lively, enthusiastic, and fond of variety as she was, the very sound of travelling had a rare charm. She who had stood on the mountains, and gazed wistfully out towards the broad world, longing to know what it was like, looked towards that distant home through rose-colored spectacles. She had never suffered. So with the trusting faith of the young, the cares and trials of every-day life to her were tinged with a roseate hue. And then, to go to America, that land above all others dear to the heart of the oppressed! For Mr. Ashton was an American, the

4

rector of a flourishing congregation in one of our largest cities. His congregation, like many another liberal one, had sent him on this pleasure trip. His wife accompanied him as far as Edinburgh, but declined taking the wild excursion through the Highlands, preferring to remain with some friends until he returned.

Had Helen been used to affection and tender care at home, she would doubtless have shrunk from parting with those around her.

Donald had never shown that he really cared for her; and his child had grown up to regard him with almost an equal degree of indifference. Her brother's disposition had likewise repelled her. She loved Margaret well; but had domineered over the old woman to too great an extent, to have for her that respect and esteem which are the only true foundation of love.

Thus it happened that, when after a two days' stay at the cottage Mr. Ashton was ready to leave, Helen bade farewell to every glen and strath and heathery mountain, every rivulet and fairy nook, with a sadness and a tenderness equalling, if not surpassing, that which she bestowed on the inmates of her home.

Old Margie wept bitterly, and sorrowed with a wild lamentation over her bairn.

"Why, I'm coming back again," said Helen, with a smile, though the tears dimmed her eyes.

"Aye, aye, ye'll come back a fine leddy, and not know old Margie," said the woman half proudly.

MacGregor's parting with his daughter was less demonstrative, but he kissed her with a warmth of feeling which surprised Helen; and turning to Mr. Ashton, he said solemnly, raising his hand towards Heaven,—

"If you forsake her, may your ashes be scattered on the water," which is the deepest imprecation of the Gael.

And so the parting was over, and Margie sighed as she went about her work, missing the light footstep and merry voice of her darling. But Helen, all unconscious that she had carried away with her the light of that cottage home, looked eagerly out at every object as they travelled on.

It was late at night when they reached Edinburgh, and Mr. Ashton found his wife anxiously awaiting his arrival. He had been detained, waiting for Helen, two days beyond his time, and they would be obliged to start the next morning.

Mrs. Ashton received Helen with a warmth and fondness for which the girl was entirely unprepared.

She held her off, and looked at her with a pleased smile, and kissed her many times, fondly calling her, "my daughter."

Miriam Ashton was a lovely woman, from whom God had deemed it wise to withhold the fond name of mother. But she was a Christian, and had learned to say the Divine prayer of the garden, "Thy will be done." And now her heart overflowed with joy and gratitude, that the Master had sent this precious lamb to her, that she might guide it to the heavenly fold.

But Helen had little time that evening to get acquainted with her new friend, for Mrs. Ashton sent her off to bed, to prepare, by a good sleep, for the morrow's journey.

They started early the next morning, and Helen was almost breathless, with a kind of awe, as she saw a large ship for the first time. It looked so huge and powerful, and the men at work on it seemed so small.

She could have staid and watched there for hours. The hurrying and bustling, raising baggage and goods, the strange shouts of the sailors, the anxious passengers, and the crowds of idle lookers on, never wearied her. But she must take her turn, and become one of the actors in the scene. And as she stood on deck, a strange sense of sorrow and loneliness came over her, as she looked towards the Highlands, and thought of her mountain home.

We will not describe the voyage. For the first week, Mr. and Mrs. Ashton were very sea-sick; and Helen spent long hours quietly sitting in their state-room, and doing all in her power to relieve them.

Or else she sat on deck, and watched with dreamy eyes the white waves dashing up to the ship; or the sailors busy at their work. She was sitting thus, one evening towards sunset, when Mr. Ashton left his state-room for the first time. He came and sat down by her.

"My dear child," he said, "you have had a lonely time of it; but now that I am better, I shall try and cheer you up. What were you thinking about, wearing such a grave face?"

Helen turned to him with a bright smile, "I believe I was a little home-sick; I was thinking

4 *

of one of Dugald's songs, and a shadow stole over my spirit."

"Can you sing it?" asked Mr. Ashton kindly. Helen commenced in her sweet, clear voice, "The Highland song of emigration."

> "'We return—we return—we return no more!'
> So comes the song to the mountain shore,
> From those that are leaving their Highland home,
> For a world far over the blue sea's foam:
> 'We return no more!'—and through cave and dell,
> Mournfully wanders that wild farewell.

> "'We return—we return—we return no more!'
> So breathe sad voices our spirits o'er,
> Murmuring up from the depth of the heart,
> When lovely things with their light depart,
> And the inborn sound hath a prophet's tone,
> And we feel that a joy is forever gone."

"Ah, Helen," said Mr. Ashton, laying his hand on the young girl's head, "you feel lonely now, yet I trust you will soon learn, that it matters little on what shore we dwell, whether the sky o'ershadows sunny vales and balmy breezes, or the ruder climes of the North. True happiness lives within the heart at peace with God. Our blessed Saviour said, when he was leaving his disciples, 'My peace I leave with you,' and since then every

Christian feels some of that divine peace dwelling in his heart, helping him to overcome the world, and to bear its trials bravely. Do you not wish to be a Christian?"

"Yes," answered Helen, a little doubtfully, for she scarcely comprehended what the term meant.

"Then pray to God to make you one, my daughter. The desire to be a Christian is the first step towards being one. If you saw a beautiful gem, and had money to buy it, you would not go to procure it unless you first wished for it. So it is with the pearl of great price, eternal life. When once you really wish for it, you will set out to seek it with earnest prayer."

"I wish," said Helen, looking wistfully down into the blue waves, "I wish we did not have to be good; it is so much easier to do just as we feel like doing."

"Yes, it is certainly easier, but I never yet saw any one, that could do just as he pleased, who was very happy. Believe me, Helen, we each of us have a life-work to do, and when we neglect that work, the sting of unfulfilled duty mars our pleasure, and instead of bringing peace and happiness renders life a burden."

"Have I a life-work, do you think?" asked Helen, thoughtfully.

"Certainly, my child, every one has his work in the great harvest field of the world; and at the last great day, each one must render up his account to the Judge of all the earth. What my Helen's work will be, time alone can show; God give her grace to do it well."

Helen sighed at the fearful responsibility that seemed thus thrown upon her. Youth dreads the thought of care and duty, and Helen almost wished she had never known that life was something more than idle dreaming through sunny days. But wish as she would, those solemn words haunted her, and she longed to know what her life-work would be.

My dear young readers, pause here, and ask what yours is. Have you already found it? or are you spending your time in the gaieties around you, without a thought of duty unfulfilled? Are there no little companions for you to lead in the heavenly road? Is there no mother's care to lighten? no father's home to cheer? no little brothers and sisters, whom you can comfort and please? If there are none of these, yet there are plenty of wandering little ones, whom you might win into the Sunday-school. Think of it, reader; you are young, perhaps, but some die young, and how will you answer the blessed Master for having neglected his work,—for having slighted duty?

Helen thought long on this, not only then, but many times. This conversation left an enduring impression on her mind, as it was the last one she ever held with her kind friend. That night typhus fever broke out on board the ship, and early and late Mr. Ashton stood at death beds, giving the consolations of religion to the dying. Then the time came when he could no longer answer to the passionate appeal for help. For he too was stricken. The shock was too great for Miriam's frail health; and with the calmness of despair, Helen bathed the brow of one, and raised the cooling draught to the lips of the other.

Oh, death, thou art indeed pitiless! The bright moon of a summer night looked down on a burial at sea. Two bodies, sewn up in coarse cloth, lay on the deck. A few sailors and passengers were grouped near them; while the captain read the solemn burial service for the dead at sea. Then the sailors gently raised the bodies. But at that moment a young girl darted from the group, and threw herself upon the dead, passionately weeping. All in vain, Helen! The deep splash is heard, a sudden stillness succeeds, and Clement Ashton and the lovely Miriam sleep in a watery grave. But why lament them? All that are in the grave shall hear his voice, and come forth, whether they rest in the "cold embrace of ocean," or sleep in the green valleys of earth. They were Christians, and for them to die was gain. Mysterious are the ways of Providence. Some writer beautifully says, "God's dealings seem to man like the scattered stones of the mosaic, valueless! It requires a master's hand to form them into a perfect picture."

Very dark and dreary seemed the world then to Helen, far away from her own home, a stranger, and alone. Yet she was not alone; God's watchful care and tenderness were over her. Ah, in that hour, how much happier would have been Helen's lot, could she have gone to her Saviour with child-like trust, and prayed him to take care of her. But this Helen had never learned to do.

She forgot her Saviour, and murmured bitterly; but He had not forgotten her. Among the passengers was a gentleman for whom Helen had often sung, during Mr. and Mrs. Ashton's illness, when she came up on deck to breathe a little fresh air. To him she imparted her simple story. He, as well as all on board, felt very sorry for her, and wondered much what would become of her. Mr. Murphy was a travelling agent, with no settled home. He felt, therefore, that he could not take care of her if he had wished, which he did not; but he had a married sister living in a small country village, to whom he determined to send Helen, if she would consent, and no better home was offered her. No one else did offer to befriend the homeless girl; and entirely ignorant of the world, without money or friends, Helen gratefully accepted Mr. Murphy's proposition. "She will do to take care of the children," thought he.

From that day Helen's brow cleared, and she felt contented once more. Youth shuns sorrow, and Helen tried to forget the true friends, sleeping in their watery grave. She and Mr. Murphy got along well together; she was never tired of hearing accounts of her new home, or stories of foreign travel, and thus many hours were whiled away, but with little profit to Helen, as Mr. Murphy was not a religious man, and Helen soon forgot the pure teachings she had learned from Mr. Ashton's lips.

Much idle time she spent in wondering what her new home would be like.

"Let me see," she would say to herself many times, "there are five children, three boys and two girls. John, Mary, Augusta, Eddie, and Charlie. Charlie, the dear little baby, how I shall love him! Indeed I'll love them all; what nice times we'll have at play, and at school! I wonder if there are any mountains or hills to climb, or heather-bells to gather?"

Thus Helen would plan and dream, and fill the future full of impossible pleasure, until she soon forgot her lost friends in the grand visions of her proud fancy. For pride was one of Helen's greatest faults, and she longed some day to return to her father's house, a rich lady. Of the treasure laid up in heaven, she never thought.

IV

THE ARRIVAL.

"Oh learn that it is only by the lowly
The paths of peace are trod ;
If thou wouldst keep thy garments white and holy,
Walk humbly with thy God."

THE whistle blew loud and long, and the great engine puffed slower, and slower, as the cars stopped at the station, and the conductor told Helen she was to get out. Poor Helen felt terribly frightened and lonely, as the cars whistled off again, and she was left standing on the platform beside her little box of clothes. She looked all around for the waiting carriage, which Mr. Murphy said would be there to meet her. For he had written an account of Helen to his sister, and told her to send to the depot for the child, as he could not accompany her. All this Helen knew, and a sickening dread came over her, at the thought that perhaps they had not got the letter. However, Helen was naturally hopeful, and as she

knew the name of the village was Brookfield, and
that it was two miles from the station, she felt certain she could get there somehow. She looked
round. No one was in sight but a man smoking
and reading a newspaper in the little room, and a
boy standing near the open door.

Helen stepped up to the boy and asked if he
knew whether there was any one there from Brookfield.

"Brookfield!" exclaimed the boy, looking surprised; "why if you wanted to go to Brookfield,
why didn't you get out at the station ten miles
above?"

"Oh, dear!" said Helen, almost ready to cry,
"is it ten miles? How shall I get there? can you
tell me?"

"Have to walk," answered the boy.

Helen stood irresolute for some time. "If it
were not for my box," she thought, "I might
walk." For Helen had been brought up in the
mountains, and miles seemed nothing much to her.

"Well, why don't you start off?" asked the boy.

"I don't know what to do with my box. Do
you think I could leave it here until they send for
it? I can easily walk the distance."

The boy looked at her in astonishment, then putting his hands in his pockets, he gave two or three whistles. "You walk it!" he exclaimed.

"To be sure I can," answered Helen bravely.

"Very well, we'll see; I'll carry your box. Go ahead."

"You go first, I don't know the way."

The boy took up the box, and walked around the house, followed by Helen. Behind the house stood a carriage and horse, and depositing the box behind, he told Helen to jump in.

Helen looked at him with some surprise, and asked, "Can we go in this carriage? Is it yours?"

The boy laughed so, he was unable to reply for some time. At length he made her understand that he had been sent to meet her. When Helen found this out, she was very angry, and refused to answer any of the numerous questions the boy put to her. But notwithstanding this, he continued to chuckle to himself every now and then, at the good joke he had played. At length Helen could endure it no longer.

"What is your name?" she asked.

"Pudding and tame," was the prompt reply.

"Now she's cross again," continued the boy,

looking mischievously into Helen's face. "You'd
better make friends with me, I tell you, for I'm
boss round our house."

This seemed so ridiculous to Helen, that she
burst into a merry laugh. This pleased the boy
so well, that he stopped teasing, and condescended
to talk sensibly. Helen soon found out that this
was John, the oldest son, but very unlike the John
she had thought about.

They were a long time getting over the two
miles; for John first drove very fast to try and
frighten Helen; then finding he could not succeed
in that, he drove very, very slow, for the rest of
the way, to try and tire her patience; and he
quite wondered to find that she did not mind it
at all.

In fact Helen was thinking a great deal too in-
tently of the kind of people of which John was a
representative, to trouble herself whether they rode
fast or slow.

At length the carriage drove up before a handsome brick house, in the main street of a small
village. A neat yard was in front filled with
flowers. As soon as the carriage drove in at the
gate, three children rushed all together out of the

front door, nearly knocking each other down in their rude haste.

"Hallo! there!" shouted John, "here we are, all safe and sound. Run in young scamps, and call your mother."

"You go, Mary."

"No, I won't; you go Eddie."

"Won't, won't," said Eddie, who was almost too small to talk plain.

"I tell you what, if some of you don't go directly, I'll get out of this carriage, with my whip. Go Gussie, run."

"Yes, go Gussie," said Mary.

Augusta, without answering, ran in, and soon reappeared with a tall, fine-looking lady. In the mean time Helen had sat patiently in the carriage and submitted to be stared at. When Mrs. Rellim appeared, she said at once,

"Why don't you open the carriage, John, and not keep the child sitting there all day?"

"Well now, mother, what's the use in my getting down just to open the door, when I will have to get right up again to drive to the stable? You open it."

"Oh, John, you are too bad; what a selfish, un-

5 *

gallant boy you are. I am really ashamed of you."

By this time Helen had succeeded in opening the door herself, and now stepped out. The children formed a regular procession to escort her up stairs; and John having utterly refused to get down and carry up the box, one of the servants was summoned from the kitchen, who with Helen's assistance took it in.

Once in the house, Helen was charmed with everything around her. Rich curtains shaded out the glaring sunlight. Her foot fell on the softest carpets. Her eye wandered with delight over pictures, books, and marble vases.

"Oh, yes," she thought, "this is the very home I've dreamed of; wealthy and beautiful. Here I shall live a fine lady, as Margie has many a time told me became a daughter of the MacGregor. Better this than wandering over the mountains, even though they be the loved Highlands of Scotland."

Thus Helen's thoughts ran on, as the children were showing her over the house. In imagination the girl saw herself reclining on the velvet sofas, dressed in silk, while her hands sparkled with jewels. Yes, as I have said before, pride was Helen's greatest fault. She was a very pretty girl, and Margie's flattering, Dugald's petting, and the pride and exclusiveness of her father, had all gone to foster her besetting sin. And yet, with this sad fault, Helen was so warm-hearted and generous, that it was often hard to chide her. She now rejoiced in this home of ease and elegance, never asking herself if the vital spirit of Christianity made it indeed a true home. She did discover, after she had been there two or three days, that every one was thoroughly selfish, each seeking to cast all duty and care on another. She found also, that no one there ever prayed or went to church, that the children were disobedient and saucy. But all this mattered little to the ease-loving Helen. She lived in a splendid home, she, as well as all the rest, did just as she pleased, and she was contented. Thus Helen would have been contented to spend her life. But thanks be to God, that he watches over us with a father's love. "And as an eagle stirreth up her nest," that her young brood may learn the use of their wings, so the Almighty Father rouses us from our slothful dreams, to teach us what life really is.

Two weeks had glided by, and Helen laughed and sang with the children, and bore John's teasing with a good nature that took away all his fun. When one afternoon, Mrs. Rellim said,

"Helen, it is so pleasant, suppose you take the children and go out for a walk; and when you come back, come up to my dressing-room, I have something to say to you."

Helen's curiosity was a little aroused, but she soon forgot it in the pleasures of the walk. She loved all nature. True, Brookfield was not her own wild home, but it had shady lanes and lovely gardens, and you could wander on to quiet woods and sunny glades where little birds sang, and the brooklet murmured.

In one of these lovely spots they sat down to rest.

"Oh, what beautiful leaves!" exclaimed Helen, looking at the fern, which grew in thick bunches.

"Shall I bring you some?" asked Gussie.

"Yes, and I'll make some wreaths for your hats."

"The first wreath is for me," said Mary.

"No, it's for me, because I got the fern. Isn't it, Helen?" asked Gussie.

"It's no such thing; I guess I'm the oldest, and I will have it."

"You shan't!" said Eddie, joining in the quarrel, and giving Mary a hit with a small switch that he carried.

Mary immediately jumped up, and struck him in the face. It took all Helen's strength, as well as powers of persuasion, to separate the two angry children; when at length they settled down, she wondered if all rich children were as ill-natured.

"I never did see such children," she said, "why can't you behave? To quarrel about such a little thing."

If Helen had been older, she might have known that nearly all quarrels are begun about some trifling thing; so trifling that people would be ashamed to tell the true cause.

"Gussie began it," answered Mary, sulkily, "and it's no business of yours; I am almost as old as you are, and we don't have to mind you."

"Gussie didn't begin it, that's a story, Mary; now I shall not make you any wreath."

"I don't want any of your wreaths; I can make a better one myself."

"You can't," answered Helen, shortly. Helen,

as well as Mary, had been brought up to have her own way, and forgetting her sage remark about the smallness of the cause, a new quarrel commenced. Not the first one they had had, for Mary and Helen could seldom agree; and continually was Mrs. Rellim bothered by complaints from Mary. But Helen was soon over her ill temper, and although Mary always sulked a while, Helen generally succeeded in getting all parties in a good humor before long. On this afternoon the beauty of the weather and all nature seemed about to be lost on the quarrelsome children. But after a while, Helen said,

"Well, never mind, what's the use in us missing this lovely afternoon? Let us all make up. I'll braid you a wreath, too, Mary."

But Mary was not to be won over for a long time. Helen tried various topics, but Mary refused to talk, until Helen asked,

"Don't you go to school, Mary?"

"Oh, yes, in winter time; it is vacation now. That is the school-house over on the hill, you see from here; oh, we have lots of fun though."

"Fun!" said Helen, looking astonished, "I thought you went there to study."

"Well, greenie! so we do, that is, we're sent there to study, but we study precious little," answered Mary.

"I'm sure I shall study when I go," said Helen.

"Are you going to school?" said Mary, in surprise; "well, you are a dunce, to go to school when you don't have to. Ma won't make you go."

"I think I'd be a dunce if I didn't go. Besides, I want to learn. Here's your wreath, Gussie, don't it look lovely?"

"I'm going to school, too, next fall, Helen, I'm so glad you're going," said Gussie, "for I shall feel so lonely among so many boys and girls. Oh, there comes Nora Neville," continued the child, jumping up, and running down the woodland path to meet a young girl carrying a pitcher. Helen looked up as they drew near, and saw Gussie with her arm around the waist of a girl several years older than herself. She had on a very pretty light chintz dress, and a straw hat; and her hair curled in little, crispy, thick curls all round the edge of it. Yet, notwithstanding a pair of bright blue eyes and rosy cheeks, Helen thought her very ugly, and she was dressed as though she was not rich; therefore, having neither beauty nor riches, she was in Helen's estimation no one of any account.

It is true Nora's nose was very pug, and her mouth not by any means small; yet those who knew Nora Neville well, generally found her nose and mouth to be entirely hidden by her pleasant smile, and white teeth. But Helen had yet to learn that there are more beautiful things in the world than a pretty face.

"Why, Nora Neville, you've been after milk," said Mary, contemptuously.

"Yes," answered the girl, looking down into the pitcher, "don't it look nice? Now if you all come round, you shall have some, for mother is going to make milk toast. Oh, I've had such a splendid walk down to Mr. Nelson's farm, and Mr. Nelson just happened to be there, and he took up the pan and filled the pitcher, although I told him it held two quarts, and I only had money to pay for one. He just called me a little witch, and told me to be off, and drink the extra milk going home. So you see I will have plenty for all hands."

"But what made you take such a big pitcher?" asked Helen, laughing at its size.

Nora, too, joined in the laugh, as she looked at it, for she had put it on the ground, "Well, mother said if the pitcher were full, I would slop it all over my clothes, I am so heedless, and would lose half the milk, and now I will show mother she was mistaken. I told her everybody would laugh at my big pitcher. But my arm is dreadfully tired. Every little stone I saw, I felt sure I'd stumble over," and Nora laughed merrily.

"My mother wouldn't let me go after milk: that's servants' work," said Mary.

"Servants' work!" repeated Nora, "so it is, when you have a servant; but we don't keep one, you know. And mother says dressing fine and doing nothing never make a lady; it is only the behaviour. But I must go now."

"No, don't go yet, Nora," said Gussie, kissing her, "I hardly ever get to see you now."

"I'd like to stay, Gussie, it is so lovely here, but mother told me not to loiter."

"What a little calf you are, Augusta," said Mary, angrily.

"I don't care," was the answer.

6

Nora took up her heavy pitcher, and they all set off together, not one offering to help her but Gussie, and she was too weak to carry it. Helen's better feelings prompted her to take the pitcher from the tired arms of Nora. But the Scotch girl, who feared nothing visible, feared the invisible, keenly felt shaft of ridicule. If Mary Rellim was too proud to carry milk, she should be too. So Nora walked on to the turning, at which she left them, merrily talking and laughing with Gussie; for Mary held herself aloof, and Helen had as much as she could do to keep Eddie in order, as he would persist in walking in the mud, and was a pitiable object when they reached home.

The walk, after they left Nora, was not very agreeable, for ill temper spoils the most pleasant thing, and Mary and Augusta were angry at each other about Nora; and Eddie was in a bad humor, because Helen would take him out of the mud. As for Helen, she felt that she had done an ungenerous and mean thing, in not offering to help Nora, and the words of the girl haunted her, "it is not how we dress, but how we behave;" and Helen felt convinced that she had not behaved at all lady-like. But with the readiness with which she usually dismissed disagreeable subjects, she said it was too late now to worry. So without taking off her things, she ran up into Mrs. Rellim's dressing-room.

V.

DARK HOURS.

"Thank God, that in life's little day
Between our dawn and setting,
We have kind deeds to give away,
Sad hearts for which our own may pray,
And strength, when we are wronged to say,
Forgiving and forgetting."

IT is a sorrowful characteristic of the human heart, that we long so earnestly to read the future. That longing is the buoy that betrays the hidden discontent of the present. But oh! wise and merciful is the "All Father" to hide every coming event, lest the shadow should eclipse the sunshine.

The woods had caught the echo of Helen's girlish laugh, as the sunlight glinted red on the tree-tops; she little dreamed then that the same woods would catch her tears, ere another hour.

As the young girl entered the dressing-room,

Mrs. Rellim looked up, and kindly asked if she had had a pleasant walk.

"Oh, very pleasant, ma'am," answered Helen.

"Perhaps you know, Helen," said Mrs. Rellim, "that when my brother sent you here, he merely sent a letter first, announcing your coming, and did not wait at all to ascertain my views on the subject. I wrote to him at once, telling him to come for you, as I could not keep you. He was absent from the city, and did not get my letter in time. Last night I received his answer. He is just about starting off again, and says it will be impossible for him to take care of you; that you must look out for another home."

All this Mrs. Rellim said in a calm, unconcerned tone, as though she was merely telling Helen to do the easiest thing in the world; while Helen listened with a flushed cheek, and averted look.

"Where can I go, ma'am!" she asked bitterly.

"I'm sure I don't know, child," Mrs. Rellim answered indolently.

"Then how am I to know?" passionately asked Helen. "Your brother deserves my warmest thanks, for taking a homeless girl, cheating her with fair promises, and then leaving her."

"There, there, child, there's no hurry about it. My brother meant kindly. Stay here a while, and inquire, and look round, and don't fret."

"Don't fret? Madam!" impatiently exclaimed the girl, while her eyes flashed with anger, "it is easy to say, don't worry, to the homeless. And this is the hospitality of America? Never a stranger sought a Highlander's cottage, but he was welcome to share the last meal. Aye, and welcome to stay till he was weary. The tongue of the Highlander would wither, ere he'd tell the stranger to go further."

"Helen! Helen!" said Mrs. Rellim, as Helen walked angrily up and down. "I do not wish you to go now. Stay as long as you wish. I only—"

"Stay now? never! I will not stay where I am not wanted."

"Listen to me, Helen,—"

But Helen had vanished. Mrs. Rellim was astonished. So merry and obliging had Helen always been, that she never dreamed of the sleeping volcano of temper that lay beneath that sunny surface. But few things ever troubled Mrs. Rellim. She sank back in her luxurious chair, saying, with a smile,

"What a little spit-fire the girl is," and resuming her book, thought no more about it.

To do Mrs. Rellim justice, she did not at all intend to turn the young girl out of her house. But she had no use for her, and did not feel obliged to keep her, merely to suit her brother's whim. All this she would have explained to Helen, had she had time. But Helen's proud, quick temper took alarm at once, and she refused to listen.

When Helen went down stairs, not caring which direction she took, so that she might get away somewhere, she rushed out of the front door, and almost mechanically took the path to the little woods. She reached the quiet spot she had left only a short time before, but twilight now rendered it gloomy. The sunlight, too, had left Helen's face, and the dark night of anger clouded it. She threw herself passionately on the ground, as she had thrown herself, many a time, in childish anger, on the wild heather, there to stay in wilful solitude, till Margaret, worried and sorry, came and coaxed her home, willingly yielding the disputed point. But no Margaret came now to soothe the spoiled girl; and Helen lay there thinking bitter thoughts of all things.

"Why had her father let her leave her own dear home, to be insulted, and turned out of doors? He might have known she would be miserable. And Mrs. Rellim,"—here her anger burst forth anew, for Helen never stopped to reason that Mrs. Rellim was under no obligation to fulfil the whims of her brother, especially as she had never even been consulted about it, or given a choice. But Helen was young and generous; and had been brought up in the lavish hospitality of a Highland home, even though a poor one. And she had inherited from her father, and been taught by Dugald, the sacred rights of the stranger. Besides all this, Helen was angry, and angry people are always unjust. Thus she chose to feel herself insulted.

"Why didn't she tell me sooner?" she continued; "to let me go on thinking I had found a home, and then to tell me I was homeless, without a moment's preparation. She is cruel; I hate her. Mr. Ashton said, when he was dying, that God would watch over me, that he had prayed for me.

He did indeed!" and Helen smiled bitterly. "My father said there was nothing in religion, and I believe it: if there is, why does God take me from a good home, to throw me alone on the world?"

Thus Helen's wicked thoughts ran on, till overcome by her desolate lot, she laid her head on a mossy stone and wept.

Poor human faith! How weak it is. How hard for it to recognize God's guiding hand in sorrow, as well as in joy.

Helen seldom cried. Light-hearted and gay, she had never, until now, known any real sorrow. But *now* she wept aloud. The sound of her sobbing went out into the still woods, and arrested the footsteps of a young girl, who was running along. She stopped and listened, then quickly drew near. It was Nora Neville. The milk toast had been partaken of with great relish; and then Nora had made a very nice extra quantity, of the remainder of the milk, and taken it to a little hut, that stood out of the village, for the supper of poor Mrs. Dales, their washwoman, and her blind boy. Now, Nora was hurrying home, as it was almost dark, when Helen's crying arrested her. She was obliged to stoop down, to see who it was. When she recognized Helen, she was very much surprised. She sat down beside her, and asked in the gentlest tone, if she could do anything for her.

" Nothing," was the cold reply.

Nora arose to go ; but hers was not the heart to leave any one in trouble. She sat down again, and putting her head close beside Helen's, she said,—

" Do tell me what is the matter, dear Helen ; perhaps I can help you."

There was no resisting such tender tones. Helen's tears ceased, as she related in an angry manner her wrongs. Now the story of Helen's coming to Brookfield, had been known in the village through the children only; and they had told that their uncle had brought Helen over for their ma. This was the story Nora had heard from Gussie ; and she now thought it very hard of Mrs. Rellim's brother to abandon Helen thus. She also thought that Mrs. Rellim might have kept her. But Nora had early been taught that God directs everything, and she was about saying so, when Helen exclaimed,

" I hate her, so I do ; I'd rather starve, than live there now."

Nora was so shocked, she almost rose up to go, but checking herself, she said,

"Oh, Helen, please don't say that; it is so wicked. The Bible says we should love everybody."

"I cannot help it. It was very heartless of her to turn me away, with no place to go to."

"Perhaps she may have had some good reason," suggested Nora, timidly.

"Some good reason!" repeated Helen, contemptuously. "If you are going to take her part, don't stay here, I'd rather not hear it."

Nora rose; she felt hurt and indignant at Helen's tone; but this feeling only lasted a moment. She remembered that Helen was angry, and did not think what she was saying; so with true Christian forgiveness, she sat down again, and said gently,

"Dear Helen, you are in trouble; mother says, when anything worries us, or we don't know what to do, we ought to ask God's help."

"He could help me without my asking him, if he wished to," gloomily answered Helen.

"Yes, he could," said Nora, "but he wishes us to ask him for what we want."

"I don't know how," was the discouraging reply.

"I know," said Nora, in a low, timid tone, "I know it seems hard at first, but it is easy, indeed it is; just kneel down and ask God to teach you what to do, to find a home, and to take care of you, for Christ Jesus, his dear Son's sake."

"Do you think he would hear me?" asked Helen, with a newly awakened interest.

"Mother says, God always listens to our prayers, if we pray in earnest, and ask the blessing for Christ's sake."

"I cannot do it," said Helen, after thinking a while. " You pray, Nora."

But this Nora could not do. Many young girls, who are truly religious, find it difficult to speak of their hopes; and almost all find it impossible to pray aloud. They are frightened at the sound of their own voices, and the simple petitions they utter to God alone, they feel ashamed of before their fellow-Christians. Nora looked troubled at Helen's request, and then she said slowly,—

"I don't think I could pray aloud, Helen, dear. But see, it is getting so dark, mother will be worried. I will go home, and tell her all about it, she will pray for you, Helen. And if you could come around to-morrow morning, perhaps mother could tell you what to do. Could you?"

"Yes, thank you, I will come," said Helen, feeling somewhat comforted that some one was taking an interest in her.

Kind words! how cheering they are; how little they cost. Why are we so chary of them?

Nora started, and then came back. "Won't you go home now? It is getting so dark."

"I have no home."

"Go back to Mrs. Rellim's then; do, please; it is so late."

All Helen's better feelings awoke, at this tender solicitude, and jumping up, she threw her arms round Nora, and gave her a hearty kiss, saying,

"You are a sweet, good girl; I love you. I will go back, even to Mrs. Rellim's, to please you."

Nora returned the embrace, and the two hastened along the road, and parted at the lane, Nora saying,

"Don't forget to-morrow morning."

When Nora reached home, she found her mother and sister at the end of the garden walk, anxiously looking for her.

7

"Oh, mother, dear, do forgive me for worrying you. I did not intend to stay so late, but I met Helen MacGregor, the Scotch girl, in the woods, and oh, mother, don't you think Mrs. Rellim has told her she must find another home, she can't keep her."

All this Nora panted forth, almost out of breath, for she had run nearly all the way home.

"There, dear child, wait a moment, until you are a little rested, and then we will hear all about it," said Mrs. Neville, kindly, "but don't stay out so late another time, for such a cause, my daughter."

"Oh, Nora, mother was so worried," said Barbara, "we were just going to look for you."

"Dear mother," said Nora, while the tears started to her eyes, and she kissed her, "I am so very sorry. But poor Helen was crying so much." And Nora then proceeded to relate Helen's account of her dismissal. But of her anger, she said nothing. Mrs. Neville had taught her children from early childhood, never to tell unkind things of any one; and to such things, the girls well knew their mother never listened.

"What do you think of it, mother?" asked Barbara. "I think it very unkind of her brother to bring Helen here, and then leave her."

"There are always two sides to a story, Barbara; perhaps Helen has done something which Mrs. Rellim thinks justifies her in dismissing her."

"Oh, no, indeed, mother; she didn't do anything," said Nora, eagerly, "she said so."

Mrs. Neville did not reply; she seemed lost in thought, which the children did not interrupt for some time, until Nora said, looking wistfully into her mother's face, "If we only could, mother."

"Yes, if we only could, Nora; I have been thinking of it, but it seems impossible."

"Thinking of what?" asked Barbara.

"Of taking Helen here," said Nora. "Don't you think we could manage it, mother?"

"Not without some self-sacrifice. You know we have only an annuity to live on, and we must not go beyond that, and we use it all at present. We might take her, indeed, if she never wanted clothes," added Mrs. Neville, smiling.

"Or, mother, if her clothes were like those of the children of Israel in the wilderness, and lasted forty years," said Barbara, laughing.

"Oh, mother, I have it," said Nora, clapping her hands, "you know you always buy us each two winter dresses, and two summer ones; now, why can't we do with one apiece, and wear our old ones longer?"

"Somehow you generally manage to wear your old ones shorter, instead of longer," said her mother, smiling.

"Well, after this, I'll try and wear mine longer," said Barbara, "if you think that will do, mother."

"That will do for *dresses*, certainly; but young girls wear shoes and stockings, and under-clothes, and hats, &c."

"Well, divide those too," said Nora, "besides, mother, you forget you will have the extra money for one dress always to buy things with; for instead of getting four dresses every time, you'll only have to buy three."

"Well, it seems you are determined to have it so. And yet, my dear girls, I do not want you to decide *now*. What you are making up your mind to, is not the work of a week, or of a month, but the sacrifice of self for years. I want you to count well the cost; there will be no retreating when Helen is once here. And you both know enough not to enter into such a pledge, without asking the guidance and help of the Giver of all good intentions, and the Upholder of all good purposes. Then, too, there will be a double watchfulness to keep over your conduct. You are Christ's children; you have become members of his visible church here on earth. In the intimate communion of daily life, you must show your young companion that you are not your own; that you have been bought with a price, even 'the precious blood of Christ,' lest you should place a stumbling-block in the way of one who will judge of Christianity by the ways of those around her. Pray earnestly for strength to do this, my daughters, and trusting in Almighty power to help, you will not fail."

Already Nora and Barbara almost felt ready to give up, at the responsible light in which their mother put it. But youth is hopeful, and as their mother sent them off to bed, they followed her advice, and prayed with sincere and simple faith, for help to sacrifice all selfishness on the altar of pure charity.

7 *

VI.

A NEW HOME.

"If we knew the clouds above us
    Held by gentle blessings there;
Would we turn away all trembling
    In our blind and weak despair?
Would we shrink from little shadows
    Lying on the dewy grass,
When 'tis only birds of Eden,
    Just in mercy flying past?"

"MOTHER dear, have you made up your mind?" was Nora's first question on the following morning.

"Have *you?*" asked her mother.

"Oh, yes, ma'am, we both have," said Barbara.

"I will tell you what I think when I get back, as I am going round to Mrs. Rellim's after breakfast."

"Why mother, I told Helen to come here."

"Did you? well then, if she comes, keep her here until I get back."

7S

"Mother, shall we go in the study, and commence our lessons?"

"No: I shall only be gone a little while, and you will have enough to do to finish the dishes, and the rest of the work."

Nora and Barbara could talk of nothing but Helen, during their mother's absence, and they laid out most delightful plans, in which everything went just as they wished, and nothing disagreeable ever entered; and they calculated largely on Helen's being a perfect character.

Mrs. Neville was a lady dearly loved in the village in which she resided, a truly noble woman; and few doors ever opened to her without a smile of welcome. Mrs. Rellim had formerly visited her; and the children, that is John, Mary and Augusta, had been almost daily visitors at Mrs. Neville's cottage. But Mrs. Neville soon found that such rude, wicked children were not just the companions for her girls. She had at first allowed them to return at long intervals the children's frequent calls; but they usually came home in such a sorry plight, from John's mischievous pranks, or from the children's quarrels, that she afterwards kept them away entirely. At this Mrs. Rellim

chose to take offence, pretending to believe that
Mrs. Neville considered her children superior to
any one else's. She dropped Mrs. Neville's ac-
quaintance, and forbade her children going there.
All this considered, it was anything but pleasant
to Mrs. Neville to call there. But self never
stood in her way when there was a duty to be
performed. She yearned over the desolate Helen,
so far from her own home; and she longed
to take her to her own warm heart; but Mrs.
Neville knew well the angry impatience of many
children; and she preferred hearing from Mrs.
Rellim's own lips whether she wished to part with
Helen, and her reasons for doing so.

The interview was cold and short. Mrs. Neville, with a Christian spirit, strove to be cordial
and kind, but Mrs. Rellim gave her to understand that a few words on the business subject
about which she had called were all that would
be acceptable.

Mrs. Neville found that everything was just as
Helen had stated it; and she determined to give
the lonely stranger a home.

Just as Mrs. Neville stepped out of the door,
she fell over a string which John had tied across

"She dropped the pitcher over as gently as possible." p. 133.

it for the express purpose of tripping her up. Providentially she did not hurt herself, only jarred her head considerably, which gave her a headache for the rest of the day. John, who was hidden behind some bushes, at a little distance, lay down on the grass and rolled over and over with laughter.

Just at that moment Helen was carrying a bucket of water into the yard, for Gussie to water her flowers with. She did not know who the lady was, but she had seen John laughing, and knew it was some of his mischief. Helen at home had always been taught politeness, and such a rude action disgusted her.

"Very well, Master John, 'it's a poor rule that won't work both ways,'" she said, as she came up to where he was lying laughing; and without a moment's hesitation she emptied the bucket of water over him. John's laughter instantly turned into anger; he jumped up and ran, but it was in vain; Helen had foreseen the consequences, and instantly throwing down the empty bucket, made for the house. She reached her room, and locked the door, just as John gave a vigorous kick against it. Notwithstanding his wet clothes, John continued at the door waiting for Helen to come out. But although Helen was very anxious to fulfil her promise to Nora, and very much worried as to what she should do, she knew John's violent temper too well to venture out until his wrath had cooled. Thus Nora waited in vain at the little gate for her expected guest.

Mrs. Rellim had promised that Helen should come round that very afternoon, if she wished to accept Mrs. Neville's offer; but she did not think it worth while to send for Helen, on purpose to tell her. So she did not mention it until dinnertime.

Helen, with the quick fancy of youth, had taken a strong liking to Nora the evening before; and it delighted her to think of living with her. Some one, it seems, really did wish for her. She had felt the whole morning as though no one cared for her, and as if everybody was anxious to get rid of her. A load was lifted from her heart.

This was the first time the children had heard that Helen was to leave; they were all surprised, and some were sorry.

"And you are going to live at Neville's?" said Mary, curling her lip, "I don't envy you. They don't keep any servant, and you'll have to run errands, as Nora does."

Helen's cheek flushed with shame, and a pain shot through her heart, as she thought, " I expect they are quite poor, and live in a mean house. I won't go live there, and have to work." But the next instant the bitter thought came that she had nowhere else to go. And she looked with regret on the splendid dining-room, and the silver and the glass on the luxuriously furnished table.

After dinner, when Helen was packing up her box, Gussie came in and slipped into her hand a very pretty copy of Robinson Crusoe.

"Take it, Helen, I'm so sorry you are going away; keep it, to make you think about me; for I'll never hardly get to see you any more."

Gussie began to cry; and the tears came to Helen's eyes as she took the book.

" I cannot read it, Gussie; you keep it."

"Oh, no, I don't want it; you will soon learn, now you are going there. Oh, but you will like it, Helen, they are all so nice; and you will be with Nora, too."

" I'm very much obliged, Gussie," said Helen, as she turned over the leaves of the handsome book; "when I learn to read it, you can come down, and we will read it together."

"Oh, I can't come and see you; ma won't let us."

Helen's cheeks again crimsoned. "It is because they are so poor," she thought; "I wish, oh how I wish, I had somewhere else to go."

Harboring such thoughts Helen was in no very good humor to look at her new home. She gazed wistfully around on every gay and handsome thing, from the rose-colored curtains to the luxurious carpet, and sighed as she looked at them for the last time.

Ah, Helen! Where were the grateful thoughts that should have filled your heart that God had not left you desolate, but had in your hour of need raised up kind friends? And then, too, were there no thanks due to the strangers who, unasked, had volunteered their help? As to the trouble and expense she might be, Helen was too little accustomed to life's responsibilities to think of them.

In the meantime, a joyful welcome was preparing for the ungrateful Helen, in Mrs. Neville's neat cottage. Barbara and Nora had a half holiday for the occasion. Helen was to occupy a room next to theirs; and busy hands had been making it as pretty as possible. There was a communicating door between the two rooms, and the girls had quite rejoiced over the fact, thinking that when they became quite intimate they could always have it open.

Barbara had tied the white curtains back with some pink ribbon, to match the ribbon in their room; and Nora had gathered all her choicest flowers into a fragrant bouquet, which, to make it look still more charming, she had placed in a white marble vase that her Aunt Stella had given her, and that usually stood in the parlor, but was now taken out to grace the dressing bureau of "Helen's room," as Nora already called it.

When everything was finished that could possibly be done, they washed and dressed themselves; and as Barbara's hair was very long and thick, Nora plaited one side, while she herself did the other, for fear they would not be ready by the time Helen came. Then they went to take a last look at the room.

"Don't it look lovely?" asked Nora.

"Yes, it does look nice," said the less enthusiastic Barbara, "of course it don't look anything like

8

as large and grand as the bed-rooms at Mrs. Rellim's, but it is so comfortable, and clean, and
pretty, that I shouldn't think Helen would care."

"Oh, she won't care," answered Nora; "why,
what's the difference *where* we sleep, if we only
sleep soundly?"

Thus saying she ran down stairs, followed by
Barbara. It was four o'clock, and the garden was
warm and sunny, so they sat down on the porch—
Barbara with a book, and Nora with some knit-
ting. Mrs. Neville had gone to see a sick neigh-
bor. The visit was one that she had wished to
pay at some time, but she chose that particular
afternoon, because she knew young girls get acquainted sooner when there are no grown people
about; and she thought if Helen were shown
around her new home by Barbara and Nora, she
would feel more at ease, and be sooner contented.

An hour passed away; Barbara had not raised
her eyes from her book; for reading was Barbara's
great passion, and even Helen, for the time, was
forgotten. Not so with Nora; she had gone down
to the gate, and looked wistfully up the road, at
least half a dozen times. She did not wish to interrupt her sister, knowing well that Barbara did

not like to be disturbed when she was reading, but after a while, she could keep quiet no longer.

"Barbara, I don't believe she is coming this afternoon,—do you?"

"Oh, yes, it is early yet."

"Early! Why it is five o'clock."

"Is it really five o'clock? I did not know it was so late. Mother will be home soon. Did you put on the tea-kettle?"

"Oh, no, I forgot it. I'm so glad you told me, Barbara."

Nora put on the tea-kettle, and Barbara went on with her book. Mrs. Neville came home, and still Helen had not come.

"Perhaps she will come to-morrow morning," said Mrs. Neville, cheerfully.

But Nora and Barbara were very much disappointed. Nora set the tea-table very quietly, with none of her usual merry comments. Mrs. Neville baked the short-cakes which were just done to a turn, as Nora, almost dropping a glass dish she held, exclaimed,

"There she is!"   .

And she was out of the room, and down the walk almost before Mrs. Neville could turn round.

With a slow step, and scanning eye, Helen en‐
tered the gravel walk. For the last hour she had
been sitting in the woods, spending her time in
useless regrets and vain murmurings at her lot.
She had bid good-bye, she said to herself, to a
luxurious life of case and wealth, and she was in
no hurry to bury herself in a poor cottage where
she would have to work like a servant. One
thing she had made up her mind to: she would
get Mrs. Neville to write at once to her father to
send for her to come home. Thus filled with rebellious thoughts, Helen's mind was lingering in
the dim old woods, as she slowly approached the
house. Nora's cordial welcome, and her evident
regret that she did not come sooner, made Helen
feel ashamed. Nora introduced her to her mother
and Barbara, and they both received her with so
much warmth and pleasure that Helen's heart
softened yet more.

Nora led her up stairs to take off her things,
and told her that that was to be her own room.
The snowy bed, and white curtains, and the sweet
breath of the flowers, all spoke to Helen of peace-
ful days and domestic joys; but her mind would
wander with regret to the room she had left.

As Helen sat down to the well-laid table, she acknowledged to herself that there was an air of refinement over everything, that was wanting in Mrs. Rellim's statelier mansion.

The table cloth was of the purest linen, the dishes white and shining. Strawberries blushed in a handsome cut-glass dish; and cake lay in delicious niceness in a silver basket. These were all relics of more prosperous days.

Helen looked round; everything was furnished tastefully and well; and even the rough fact of baking cakes Mrs. Neville performed with a lady-like grace that astonished Helen, accustomed as she had been to the coarse manners of the servants at Mrs. Rellim's.

When supper was over Nora almost hid herself in a large check apron, which fastened around the neck with a string, and came down to the bottom of her dress. She laughed merrily as she looked down at herself, and Helen joined in the laugh.

"You see," said Nora, "it is my week in the kitchen, and so I am going to wash the dishes now," and she proceeded to pour water out of the kettle into the dish pan.

8 *

Mrs. Neville took the work basket and commenced darning some stockings, and Barbara sat
down in the open door-way. The merry manner
in which Nora went to work seemed to take away
the fact that it was work at all. Helen expected
to be disgusted with the "servants' work," as she
imitated Mary Rellim in saying, but she found
herself laughing quite as heartily as the rest, when
Nora, in her excitement, wiped a dish carefully,
and then put it back in the pan of water!

When all was finished, Nora took off her apron,
and with Helen and Barbara went into the garden.

First they visited the flower garden in front of
the house,—a perfect wilderness of beauty. Roses
bloomed on all sides, from the crimson petals of
the damask, to the snowy blossoms of the acacia.
Heliotrope, sweet alyssum, mignonette, white lilies,
and the sweet brier laded the air with perfume.
Helen was delighted. She loved flowers in-
tensely; and as she bent over to inhale their
sweetness, tears sprang into her eyes. Helen once
again saw the green hills of her own dear land.
Oh, the subtile power of a perfume to carry memory back to sunny haunts of other days! Helen's

heart went forth in vague, wild yearnings for her absent home.

Nora and Barbara saw the tears, but were too considerate to notice them in words; only Nora gently put her arm around her, and said, gaily,

"This is my bed over here, and that is Barbara's. Mother lets us plant just what we wish."

It was curious to note the difference in the two flower-beds. Barbara's contained only a few flowers, but those were very choice; while Nora's held in it a little of everything. There was some chick-weed in one corner, because Nora always supplied the birds in the village with it; a few flowers and various kinds of herbs which Nora dried and put away in bundles, because poor people were always wanting them.

After Helen had duly admired all these, they went to the vegetable garden at the back of the cottage. Here Mrs. Neville usually raised all the vegetables necessary for their own use. Her husband had been a physician, with a lucrative practice; but cut off suddenly in early life by an epidemic fever, he had left only a small annuity to support his wife and two children. Mrs. Neville had moved into this small cottage, and by strict

economy managed to keep a comfortable home.
Mr. Nelson, their landlord, a rich bachelor who
had been an intimate friend of her husband's, sent
his own gardener each spring to prepare the
ground and plant the vegetables, as well as to
superintend it once in a while. Helen not knowing this, was surprised at the size and perfection
of everything; and she was just going to ask about
it, when Mrs. Neville's voice was heard calling
them to come in.

It was the time for evening worship. Mrs.
Neville read a chapter in the Bible, and they all
knelt down while she offered a fervent prayer.
In that prayer Helen was not forgotten. Thanks
were given to God for having found a home for
the stranger. Earnest supplication was made that
they might all live happily together as a Christian
family; and that Helen might ere long be gathered
as a lamb to the fold of Christ.

When Helen retired that night, the room and
its contents were forgotten in the recollection of
that solemn prayer. For the first time in her life
she thought seriously of God and religion. Could
it be possible, she thought, that it was the great
God who had found that home for her? "Ah,"

she continued aloud, "old Margie would say it was my good luck; but Mr. Ashton said there was no such thing; I wonder which is right? *They* are. I feel they are; it must have been God directed me here. And I—I'm sure I did not want to come. I do not want to stay. Mrs. Neville told me to thank him to-night; but I will not, I am not contented."

Helen went to the looking-glass and began taking down her hair; she smiled back at the pretty face it reflected; but all she could do she could not avoid hearing the whispers of conscience, nor still the cry of an awaking spirit.

While these thoughts were passing through Helen's mind, Barbara and Nora in the next room were also preparing for bed.

"What do you think of her, Barbara? Isn't she lovely?"

"Yes, she is very pretty; she puts me in mind of the picture of Grace Hawthorne, in the Sunday-school book we were reading."

"Oh, she is much prettier than the picture of Grace, for don't you remember Grace looked as if she had crooked eyes, and how we laughed at it? I wonder if Helen is as good? I wonder if she'll blot her copy-book, or lose her slate-pencils as I do," continued Nora, sitting on the floor in her night dress, with her hands clasped round her knees.

"Nora, you've not read yet; and you know mother don't like us to keep the light burning."

"Oh, I forgot," said Nora, jumping up and taking her little Bible, "I guess she'll be like you Barbara, so careful."

"Hush, Nora, how can I read?"

"Just one question, Barbara, dear; you know after I have read and said my prayers, I can't speak. Do you think she'll ever wear her Scotch dress?"

Barbara made no answer, and with a sigh of disappointment Nora opened her Bible and began to read. But she was not as attentive as usual that night; and even after they were in bed she broke one of her mother's rules by whispering the question again to Barbara. Barbara only gave her a push with her arm, and Nora, sorry for having spoken, turned over, and tried to sleep.

VII.

THE DORCAS SOCIETY.

"I would not that life's changing sky
    Should know no cloudy weather,
That shadows fall not on the heart,
    But sunlight altogether;
The blossoms on the brow of May
    Are born of April showers,
And shall we be too wise to learn
    A lesson from the flowers?"

SEVERAL days passed away, and Helen was beginning to feel more at home. She found that in this well-appointed household, each one had her own special duties; and that everything was systematized in such a way, that all had time for work and play. Mrs. Neville carried out strictly the old saying, "a place for everything, and everything in its place." Which, simple rule that it is, has saved many a fit of ill humor and impatience.

Mrs. Neville had given Helen a small Bible,

95

exactly like Barbara's and Nora's, and a flower
bed like theirs also. Of this last, Helen thought
and cared much more than she did of the former.
Each morning during those long warm days
of summer, the dressing-bell rang at five o'clock.
One week Nora washed the dishes, set the table,
and helped her mother in the kitchen, while Barbara made the beds, and attended to the up stairs
work. The next week Barbara took the down
stairs work, and Nora the up stairs. Then, whose-
ever week it was up stairs, weeded in the garden half an hour before breakfast, which they
ate at six o'clock. At half past eight, school
opened. Back of the parlor was a cheerful room,
fitted up as a school-room, and called the study.
The green carpet, green blinds, and book-case, had
once been in Dr. Neville's office. Mrs. Neville
had put them in the school-room, thus giving it
very much the appearance of a study.

Mrs. Neville was a highly educated woman, and
she preferred teaching her girls herself to sending
them to the school on the hill. Here the morning
hours were passed until twelve o'clock, when
school was over for the day. At one o'clock they
took dinner; and from twelve to one, either Bar-

bara or Nora practiced her music lesson. From two to three was the study hour. From three to four they sewed. Each one made and mended her own clothes, with Mrs. Neville's assistance and direction; from four, until bed-time, they could do as they pleased. This, Helen soon learned, was the regular order of the day.

So far she had not been asked to do anything, and it pleased her well. To be sure she did feel ashamed sometimes, and had almost made up her mind to offer to help; but she was still thinking about it. She had been given her seat in the study, provided with books, and had commenced studying with an alacrity that pleased Mrs. Neville.

Everything had gone on very smoothly; the girls were finding all their pleasant anticipations realized, and were learning to love Helen very much, and to think her very good.

One morning as Helen awoke, and saw the sun shining into her room so brightly, she jumped hastily up, saying,

"I wonder if the dressing-bell has rung yet? It is Saturday morning."

But her doubts were instantly dispelled by a fu-

9   G

rious ringing, and Nora's merry voice calling out,

"Dressing-bell! Dressing-bell!"

Helen put her head out of the door to join her laugh, and cry as they used to on board the boat,

"Gentlemen who have not paid for their tickets, will please step up to the Captain's office and settle." Then she quickly withdrew her head, as Nora pretended to throw the bell up at her.

"What a sweet canny darling Nora is," thought Helen, as she was dressing, "she turns all her tasks into happiness. Now it is her week in the kitchen, and she often has to give up some play that she enjoys very much, to go and set the table, or get the milk, and she never seems to mind it at all. Yes, there must be a great deal in religion. She finds so much comfort in her prayers and texts, while they are nothing to me; perhaps I shall learn some day," and with a sigh half merry, half sad, Helen finished dressing. Then she put the bed-clothes on a chair to air, and opened the window.

"There," she exclaimed, "I believe that is just as Barbara told me," and she turned again to the window, and drank in the sweet morning air, laden with perfume, and filled with the melody of birds.

"Oh, how I wish there was nothing in the whole world to do but to lie down under green trees, and listen to the birds sing, to live on the breath of roses, and idle away long summer days in mossy dells, and beside sparkling waters. Why must life be full of work and study?"

Helen thus dreamed away her morning half hour, and was only roused by Barbara's voice singing in the parlor below. Helen ran down quickly, and burst into a merry laugh, as Barbara, with her head tied up in a towel, and a dust-pan in her hand, met her in the entry.

"Well, Barbara, I find you are one of the early birds this morning."

"You know it is Saturday," said Barbara, "and I've swept the parlor already; now, while I'm eating my breakfast, the dust will be settling nicely."

Helen looked at her with a smile and a sigh. The smile was for Barbara's industry, the sigh for her own idleness.

After breakfast Mrs. Neville asked Helen if she would please wash the dishes, as Barbara was dusting the parlor, Nora sweeping the kitchen, preparatory to scrubbing it, and she herself was going to market.

Helen answered, "Yes, ma'am," but Mrs. Neville noticed with sorrow the flush of annoyance on her cheek, and her discontented look. She had undertaken the charge of Helen, and she wished to bring her up exactly as she would if she were her own daughter. She had allowed her several days to get accustomed to things; but now she wished her to begin, well knowing Helen would feel more at home when once she took her share in the domestic affairs.

Mrs. Neville took no notice of Helen's ill humor, but went out. As soon as she had gone, Helen sat down to indulge her angry thoughts. "She didn't like to work," she said to herself, "she hated it, and she didn't intend to be forever doing it."

Nora peeped her curly head in at the door for a moment, to ask how she was getting along. But seeing Helen seated and looking so glum, she asked what was the matter.

"Nothing," answered Helen coldly.

"Dear Helen, it must be something. Can I help you?"

"You can please leave me alone," was the ungracious answer.

Nora shut the door, and the tears stood in her eyes at Helen's unkind manner. This was the first cloud that had dimmed their pleasure since Helen's arrival. Nora remembered her mother's caution, and kneeling down in the kitchen she said a short prayer, asking God to help Helen, and to give to her own heart grace to overlook all unkindness.

When Helen heard Mrs. Neville's voice in the kitchen, some time afterwards, she commenced washing the dishes, and having finished them, she went up to her own room to put it in order. But instead of coming down, she lingered there, spending her time in idle wishing.

When she came down to dinner no one made any comment on her absence or ill humor; all treated her just as kindly as ever. Helen, with all her faults, was really a warm-hearted girl, and this kindness and forbearance touched her deeply. She felt so ashamed that she longed to acknowledge her wrong, and to make amends, but pride kept her silent. Helen felt very much dissatisfied with herself, and so more out of humor than ever.

"This is Dorcas afternoon," said Barbara.

9 *

"Oh, so it is," said Nora, "and I can finish the little pair of drawers I am making."

" What is Dorcas afternoon?" asked Helen.

Nora proceeded to tell her, that every Saturday afternoon the girls in Mrs. Neville's Bible-class met there to sew for an hour, from half past two to half past three, for the poor in the village.

"You see," said Barbara, "we keep our sewing circle all the year round, because ours is not like most Dorcas societies, since we only furnish part of the material. But if any of the poor families have clothes to make for themselves, and can't find time, or don't know how to do it, why they bring them to us."

"That is a very easy way to get rid of work," said Helen. "I think I shall send mine in too."

"Oh, but we don't make anybody's clothes, unless mother knows that it is impossible for them to do them themselves. Now there was poor Mr. Dean. Last winter his wife died, and left six children, and he could not afford to hire a housekeeper; so his eldest daughter Lucy, only fourteen, had to take care of the house and children; and of course mother knew she couldn't make her father's shirts and the children's clothes. So our little Dorcas sewed for her all last winter. And we do yet, sometimes, although Lucy is getting very handy," said Barbara.

"But I shouldn't think you could get much done in an hour," said Helen.

"Many hands make light work," said Nora; "mother has eight girls in her class, and Barbara and I make ten, and mother eleven, and mother is nearly equal to a sewing machine, and now you will be twelve."

Helen did not reply, but she made up her mind that she was not going to trouble herself to hurry. She had to sew on her *own* clothes every afternoon, during the sewing hour, and she thought that was enough.

It is wonderful what little things vex and provoke us, when we are in an irritable humor. When Helen entered the parlor, ten minutes after the time, she found the whole sewing circle busily at work. It would have pleased almost any one to see those ten young girls, all laughing and talking, while their fingers flew backwards and forwards over hem or seam. Mrs. Neville introduced Helen, and then told her to select a piece of work out of a large basket which stood in a corner.

Helen took a small pink apron, which had been cut out of an old one of Nora's.

"Why, Helen," said Nora, laughingly, "I believe you picked out the smallest piece there."

Many of the girls joined in the laugh, but Helen, instead of taking it in fun, as it was intended, chose to feel still more out of humor. Then too, she was provoked that Nora should sit by a pale, poorly-dressed girl, and take so much trouble to entertain her. Helen thought she might have come and talked to her, as she was a stranger there. She did not know that this was Lucy Dean, who seldom enjoyed anything, from being so poor, and having the constant care of her little brothers and sisters; so that when she came there Nora tried to make it pleasant for her. But in a few minutes the talking ceased, and Mrs. Neville read them a short but interesting story. The story was of a man who was very intemperate, but who was reclaimed through the earnest Christianity of his young daughter.

Helen sat thinking about it; her anger was fast changing into sorrow. Nora noticed that Helen looked unhappy, and leaving Lucy she came and sat down by her side.

"How did you like the story, Helen?" she asked.

"I didn't like it at all," answered Helen shortly.

"You didn't like it!" exclaimed Nora, in surprise; then seeing Helen's cheek flush painfully, she said softly, "Dear Helen, you are unhappy. What is the matter?"

"Well," said Helen, frankly, "I'm in a bad humor. First I was provoked at everybody, and now I am provoked at myself."

"But that had nothing to do with the story, Helen; why didn't you like that?"

"Because no one *could* be that good. When Melinda's father got drunk and beat her, she just went away without saying a word and prayed for him. I don't believe it. I would not have staid with him, or if I had to, I would never have let him beat me; and I'm sure no one could feel like blessing another, after behaving that way."

"I know," said Nora, "it must have been very hard, and she could never have done it of herself; but Jesus gave her strength."

"Now really, Nora, do you think God intends us never to resent our injuries? Suppose some one was to come here, and insult me; I think I would be foolish to sit down quietly, and not pay him back."

" Why, Helen dear, didn't you know we are told in the Bible to follow our blessed Saviour's example in all things? And I'm sure we'll never be called on to bear half the sufferings he endured."

" But he was God," said Helen, "and he could bear them better."

" But mother says he bore them as a man, in his human body, and suffered as much as if he had not been God. I know not very long ago a girl took one of Barbara's books; and she would rather lose anything, almost, than a book; so she went after it, and the girl told her she hadn't it, and just shut the door in her face. When Barbara came home, she was very angry. Mother talked to us a long time about bearing little things. And I remember she said, that the best way for us to learn to bear our little troubles and disappointments patiently, was always to stop and think how much Jesus bore. Just to think, Helen," and the tears started to her eyes, "that they actually slapped him, and spit in his face, and made fun of him, besides scourging him, crowning him with thorns, and at last crucifying him,—and all for us."

"And just to think," said Helen, "He was God, and might have destroyed them at once."

"Yes," said Nora, "and yet he only prayed for them. Even on the cross he prayed to God to forgive them. And mother says he gives us some of his strength to endure and forgive, if we only pray for it aright. And so you see, Helen, that was why the girl in the story could do it."

"Yes, I suppose she could do it, and so could you, Nora, but I never could."

"Oh, yes, indeed you could, Helen, if you asked Jesus' help, as Melinda did."

"Well," said Helen, slowly, "*perhaps* I might; but I'm not like you and Barbara. I hate to be useful; when I was at home I never did anything, unless I pleased, and now I like to waste my time; and this morning, when your mother asked me to wash the dishes, I got angry, and when I get angry everything makes me worse; I shall never learn to be good. If I were only like you and Barbara!"

"Don't say that, Helen; you have no idea how heedless I am. But mother says, no matter what our faults are, Jesus can give us grace to conquer them."

"Ah," said Helen, "if I only could. You make me long to be a Christian."

"Do, do be one, Helen dear; mother says that is the first step in our life-work. For how can we go and work in the Saviour's harvest-fields, unless we are his servants?"

"Life-work!" repeated Helen slowly. "Ah, I remember, that calm moonlight night on the ocean. Beauty everywhere around us. Yes," continued Helen musingly, and speaking more to herself than to her companion," yes, he said I had a life-work to do, and I remember shrinking from the thought. I said to myself, I would rather live on as joyously and unconsciously as a butter-fly. But I see there is something more in life than mere pleasure,—a higher aim, a sweeter joy. If Mr. Ashton were alive, how I should like to tell him that I understand him better now."

"Mr. Ashton!" said Nora, "on board of a ves-sel! Why, were you on board the same vessel, coming from Europe, that my uncle Clem was?"

"Your uncle!" said Helen, "was the Rev. Clement Ashton your uncle?"

"Yes," said Nora sadly, "dear uncle Clem and aunt Miriam both died at sea. That is why mother is so quiet, and the tears often fill her eyes; he was her only brother, and we all loved him so. Did you know him well?" and Nora bent down over her sewing to hide her tears.

Helen was astonished; she commenced relating, in a hurried manner, Mr. Ashton's visit to the Highlands, and her own departure with him. The conversation was interrupted by the breaking up of the sewing party, and Nora left Helen to help the girls on with their things, and to bid them good-bye. But when the last one had gone out of the garden gate, Nora told the news. They were all surprised. This was the first time they had heard the true version of Helen's emigration. The girls, instead of going to the woods, as they had intended, spent the afternoon with their mother, listening to Helen's account of Mr. and Mrs. Ashton. Many tears were shed over the loved brother and uncle, and the gentle aunt Miriam. And Mrs. Neville clasped Helen to her heart, and said she should indeed be a daughter to her.

She felt as though God had directed Helen

10

there, that she might fulfil, as far as she could, her brother's promises.

She also told Helen, that on Monday she would write to Scotland, and inform her father of all that had happened.

When Helen went to bed that night, she felt happier than she had felt for a long time. The love and kindness of the Neville family, and their deep religious principles, were influencing her heart and mind. She longed to be like them; and she knelt and prayed to God to teach her to live a better life.

Then, too, Nora and Barbara seemed to her almost like sisters now, since she was to have been the adopted daughter of their uncle.

For the first time since she came there, Helen lay down in her comfortable bed, with no thought of its simple neatness contrasting with the grandeur of Mrs. Rellim's.

VIII.

THE DAY OF REST.

"And sweetly over hill and dale
    The silvery sounding church bells ring;
  Across the moor and down the dale
  They come and go, and on the gale
    Their Sabbath tidings fling."

HOW very different our evening thoughts appear to us, in the broad light of the morning. Perhaps we have spent the night in fear and anxiety, but the cheerful sunlight inspires confidence and hope. It sometimes seems as though one of the great missions of night was to make us pause and think, undisturbed by the many distractions of the day. But, alas, it often happens that the good resolution of the night, like the dew, evaporates in the genial warmth of daylight. When Helen went to bed the night before, she felt as though all in the house had attained to a Christian life which she feared she could never

imitate, and she had prayed for help to live better.
When she arose in the morning, her fear of the
evening before had gone.

" If they are kind and obliging to me," she
thought, " I can return it surely. I love them,
and it cannot be a hard task to oblige those we
love. What would Margaret think? She used
always to say I was the brightest blossom in the
Highlands; what would she think, did she know,
there are others here whose words and actions put
her own Helen to shame? No," continued Helen,
and she looked into the glass, and threw back her
head, with a gesture worthy of her father, " No, a
Highland girl must never be outdone in kindness."

Poor, foolish Helen! Striving to stand on the
sandy foundation of her own weak will. The
great defect in Helen's character, was the want of
a guiding principle. She loved to admire, and
dream of great purposes, and noble deeds, but
when the moment came to perform them, she sank
back into selfish indolence. She liked to do kind
and generous things, when they cost her little
trouble; but even then, she did them without any
discrimination, and bestowed her money as readily

for a bad as for a good cause, if it happened to touch her feelings. She never stopped to ask herself the questions, "Is it right? Will it please God?" Of all this, old Margaret never thought, how then should Helen know? Thus she began that week on the wrong principle. Very true Helen had prayed, the night before, for strength and guidance; but she only wished to imitate the daily life around her, which she admired. No deep sorrow for her pride and unthankfulness and many sins, sent her a lowly penitent to the foot of the cross; and until then, she must walk on in darkness, vainly struggling for the light.

She went to Sunday-school and church with Barbara and Nora, and began her first week of work, true to her good resolution, with a promptitude that pleased Mrs. Neville. Helen was very well satisfied; she took "a ray of sunlight for an abiding day," and came to the conclusion that to be a Christian only needed a firm determination to do right.

"Oh, dear, what shall I do?" said Nora, in a distressed tone, coming after dinner into the study where Barbara was reading her library book,

10 *   H

and Helen was looking over the pictures in the large Bible.

"What is the matter?" asked Helen.

"I cannot find my Bible," answered Nora, beginning to go round the room, and turning up everything she came to.

"Don't make such a noise, please, Nora," said Barbara; "it was so cool and quiet in here, I was just saying it seemed like Sunday. Your book can't be in here; you have not been in this room to-day, before."

"No, I know I wasn't, but then it might have got in here, for my things get everywhere. I'll try and not make a noise, Barbara dear."

"I'll help you look for it," said Helen, getting up, "if you want it now; but there are two Bibles on the book shelf, why don't you read in one of those?"

"Oh, yes, I know there are plenty of Bibles," said Nora, knocking down three books in her search; "but see, it is nearly a quarter of three o'clock, and at three mamma will be in, for it is our lesson hour, and she always wants us to use our own Bibles. Oh, I do wish I did not forget so."

"Why, do you have a lesson on Sunday?" asked Helen, looking surprised.

"Oh, a Bible lesson. You will like it, Helen; mother always gives us some man or woman in the Bible to study about, and then we learn all we can of them, and mother questions us, and talks to us about them."

"Take my Bible," said Helen, "you know it is just like yours, and your mother will never notice."

"Oh, Helen, how can you? Why that would be deceiving mother, and acting a story."

Helen drew back slightly offended, and said pettishly, "Well, even if she did know it, I don't see why she would care. One Bible is just as good as another."

"Yes, so it is. But mother says if we keep our own Bibles, and always use them, they become so dear to us after a while, that we love them, and love to read in them, and get used to finding all the places."

"Really, Nora, I can't make any sense of what I'm reading, you talk so," said Barbara; "your Bible can't be in here."

"No, it isn't in here; I'll go out and look in

the parlor once more, though I'm sure I have looked everywhere."

Nora searched in the parlor, the kitchen, and the porch, and Helen followed.

"Do try and think what you did with it, when you came in from church; I saw it in your hand then," said Helen; "where did you go first?"

"I just came in, and went up stairs, and took off my hat and mantle, and put on my apron, and came down here on the porch, and sat until dinner time."

"Did you look up stairs?"

"Oh, yes, I looked all over, and shook out my mantle too. But come, we must go in now, it is almost three, and mother will be down directly."

"Take my Bible," insisted Helen.

"I would not care so much," continued Nora, with a sigh, and without answering Helen, "only I have been trying so hard lately not to forget where I put things, and now mother will think I have gone back already."

"Take my Bible," again said Helen, as they reached the study door.

Nora made no answer, and Helen indignantly thought, "There, I don't see any use in my trying

to behave better. I try to oblige Nora, and she
all but tells me I am acting wickedly. I don't
see any use in being so very good about trifles. I
can't be good where people are so full of notions.
Well, never mind, I'll not be discouraged; I'm
improving, anyhow, and I don't intend to be outdone by Nora."

Alas, Helen did not know she could never improve while she trusted to her own guidance and
strength. Nor indeed did she succeed entirely in
deceiving herself. She secretly admired the firm
principle in Nora's life, which made her shun the
wrong at once; but that only added to her desire
to live as Nora did. Helen had yet to learn that
it is no true kindness to lead another into temptation. Many girls would have yielded to her
entreaties; and thus Helen would have been the
cause of their deceiving, all through her mistaken
notion of being good. But Nora was a Christian
child, and said her prayers too faithfully and
earnestly, to be so easily led astray. She did not
answer Helen again, but opened the study door,
and took one of the Bibles off the shelf, and sat
down to find the lesson. Barbara also laid aside
her book, and took her Bible. Helen drew a

chair to Nora's side, as Mrs. Neville opened her door, up stairs, preparatory to coming down.

"Why, what is in your pocket, Nora?" said Helen, "I hit my hand quite hard against it."

Nora put her hand into her pocket, and they all smiled, as she drew forth the missing Bible. The amusement was scarcely over, when Mrs. Neville entered the room.

These Sunday afternoon lessons were heartily enjoyed, both by mother and children. It was a pleasant picture, the quiet shady room, Mrs. Neville, still fulfilling the promise of her girlhood in her matronly beauty, sitting by the open window, which gave a glimpse of green grass, golden with the warm sunlight, through which came the sweet song of birds, and the perfume of the flower garden. And Helen's eyes wandered more than once to the bright landscape beyond. Then those youthful forms, bent over their open Bibles, with "their yet unwritten brows," learning to tread in the narrow road which leadeth unto eternal life.

"What is the character for to-day, Barbara?" asked Mrs. Neville.

"Absalom."

The lesson then began. Barbara told all that was known of the first part of his life; that he was David's favorite son, that his mother's name was Maacah, and how beautiful he was. Then Nora took it up, and continued,

"He had one sister, whom he loved very much, named Tamar. His brother Amnon injured her, and Absalom was very angry with him. He made a great supper at the time of sheep-shearing, and invited all his brethren. They all accepted the invitation, excepting Amnon. Then Absalom asked his father David to compel Amnon to come. Amnon came, and Absalom told his servants to fall on him and kill him, which they did. For this, Absalom was banished from Jerusalem."

"He was in exile two years," said Barbara, "and then Joab employed a wise woman of Tekoah to go and plead with David, and to represent Absalom's case, as though he had been her own son; and she begged the king that he might be restored from banishment."

"What did the king say, Nora?" asked Mrs. Neville.

"David perceived that she meant Absalom, and he asked at once if Joab had not sent her? The woman said, yes, and the king allowed Absalom to return to Jerusalem, but did not see him for two years."

"After this," said Barbara, "Absalom behaved very badly to Joab. He burned his grain-fields, because Joab did not get him restored to the presence of the king his father. After that, Absalom was permitted to go to court."

"When Absalom had been in Jerusalem some time," said Nora, "he got himself many chariots and horses, and servants to run before him. Then by his beauty and flattery, he stole the hearts of the children of Israel away from David his father, and he went to Hebron, and had himself proclaimed king there."

"Go on, Barbara," said Mrs. Neville.

"The rebellion lasted some time, and David was obliged to flee from Jerusalem. But he gave charge to all the people, and to the captains of his host, that if they took Absalom, they were to spare his life, and deal gently with him. The followers of Absalom were defeated; and Absalom was running away, when the mule on which he rode ran under the thick branches of an oak tree, and Absalom's head was caught in the branches; the mule went from under him, and left him hanging there."

"Some of the men saw him," said Nora, "and they told Joab, and he went and thrust a dart through him, and killed him. David lamented very bitterly over the death of his favorite son."

Helen had been deeply interested in this story. There was a daring recklessness about Absalom, that suited well her wild fancy. She forgot his deep sins, and base ingratitude to a fond father, and she was thinking so deeply of his shameful death, that she almost started when Mrs. Neville said,

"There are so many lessons, so many warnings in the life of Absalom, and our hour is so nearly gone, we will only have time for a few remarks now, and take the lessons to be drawn from it for next Sunday afternoon. One point I would specially mention,—the warning against vanity. Fearfully does the story of Absalom teach, that beauty is a great snare unless it is consecrated to the service of God. Absalom's beauty won him the hearts of Israel, and led to his dark sins. But the principal lesson I wish you to learn from this is the uncertainty of life, and the necessity of being pre-

pared for death. The wise man says, "There is a
time to die." A time for every one that lives to
become even as Absalom. And I was thinking
how strikingly this death of Absalom teaches us
that nothing earthly can save us from the doom
of all. Absalom was the son of a king, and so
stood high among men. He was very wealthy;
we are told he had several thousand chariots,
horses, and servants. He was very beautiful.
He was deeply loved by his father, and by all
Israel. More than that, he was young. And yet
he died. Nothing earthly could save him; neither
wealth, nor greatness, nor beauty; not the fond,
doting love of a father, who was one of God's
chosen; not the strength and vigor of his youthful
manhood, nothing. It had come his time to die,
as it will come ours; and, oh, then, my dear children, happy are they who have the Saviour's arm
to lean upon; who have a Saviour's hand to
smooth a dying pillow. Did you ever lie awake
at night, and think, suppose I should die to-night,
to what place would I go? Would I have the
blessed Saviour to lead me gently through the
dark waters up to the eternal gates of pearl?
Dear girls, nothing grand, or great, or beautiful,

that earth bestows, could save Absalom; and
nothing earthly will avail *you* in that solemn hour.
Then pray each day more earnestly for faith and
love. Lay up treasure in heaven; so, when the
Master cometh, at midnight, or at the cock-crow-
ing, he shall find you ready."

Mrs. Neville ceased, and tears dimmed the eyes
of her youthful listeners. When she left the room,
quietness reigned in the little study. Each one
was thinking, in her own way, of Mrs. Neville's
words, "you, too, must die." And to each one,
how differently came the thought.

Barbara thought at first of the dread of dying;
but she soon remembered stories she had read of
children who had died happy, and she gradually
wandered away in fancy, to her own tomb, when
she should be dead; and how her mother and
sister, perhaps, would kneel and weep over her,
till in the fancy picture she forgot the solemn preparation and the life hereafter.

Not so Nora. With sweet childish faith,
she believed that her Saviour was ready to welcome her. Had he not said, "Suffer little children, and forbid them not to come unto me: for of
such is the kingdom of heaven?" She had gone

to him, with all her sins and weaknesses. She loved him, and a sweet peace settled on her heart as the beautiful words of the hymn came into her mind,

"Fear not, I am with thee; O be not dismayed!
 For I am thy God, and will still give thee aid;
 I'll strengthen thee, help thee, and cause thee to stand,
 Upheld by my righteous, omnipotent hand."

She stole quietly up to her own room, there to kneel once more and hold sweet communion with her Saviour.

But of what was Helen thinking? How came the solemn warning to the gay Scotch girl? She leaned her elbow on the table, and her head in her hand, and gave herself up to deep thought. She was troubled to the very depths of her soul, with a vague yearning and unrest. A vision of her own native land swept over her,—its lone mountains and wild moors, where, free and careless, she had followed her own gay will, without a shade of care. No one there had troubled her with thoughts of dying. No one had urged her to love a crucified Redeemer; and she longed to be back again, treading with light, free footstep the mountain side. And yet, through all this longing, a still small voice was whispering, " there is a higher life; you must live forever, either in happiness or in misery." She had not lived even for that short time, in the heart of a truly Christian family, without feeling that there must be a life beyond. Their actions were guided by rules of which she knew nothing.

But sadness was not pleasing to Helen. She soon began to think more cheerfully. She glanced into the looking-glass. Her dark curls swept a cheek rosy with health, and giving her head a gay shake, she smiled, as she thought, " Why should I worry? I am young and healthy, and life is very pleasant. Besides, I would never be as wicked as Absalom was."

Stop, Helen! Look into your heart. Are you not, even now, rebelling against God, your heavenly Father—refusing to submit to his will in all things? Have you not been ungrateful for his many favors? Even now, do you not look into the glass with some of Absalom's vanity? Vanity, ingratitude, rebellion! Are Absalom's sins *yours*, my reader? Oh, think how earthly pride and vanity must appear in the holy presence

11 *

and splendor of Him before whom the angels veil
their faces!

Does ingratitude whisper in your heart a discontent with a humble home? or with the all-wise
dealings of the God who gives you all things, even
the very air you breathe? Oh, if such be your
case, rebel no longer against One before whom rebellion is impotent, and yet who condescends to
entreat your love and fealty,—who gave his **only**
Son, to win you back to love and **life.**

THE BROKEN PITCHER.

"One by one thy duties meet thee;
 Let thy whole strength go to each:
 Let no future dream elate thee;
 Learn thou first what these can teach."

WEEKS glide rapidly by when busy hands
and light hearts help them on their way.
Helen was still struggling on in her pride and self-
will, striving to attain to a Christian life without
the help of the great Guide. She was like a blind
man walking on the verge of a precipice, who re-
fuses to listen to the friendly voices around him
urging him out of danger, and who heeds not the
hand stretched out to succor him. Thus Helen
lived week after week, and listened to Mrs. Neville's earnest prayers and teachings without pro-
fiting by them. She strove to still the murmurings of an awakened spirit by the performance of
good deeds. Hers was a gay, lively disposition,
and when conscience whispered, she drowned the

127

still small voice in some funny prank or amusing play. She took her turn in the household duties without repining outwardly, but inwardly she still longed for the wealth and ease of Mrs. Rellim's. Her happiest hours were spent in the school-room. There she learned with a rapidity that surprised Mrs. Neville. Barbara, with her mother's consent, had borrowed Helen's copy of Robinson Crusoe. As she finished reading each chapter, she related it to Helen. The longing wish to read as well as Barbara read, gave an additional impulse to Helen's study hours. Helen was naturally impatient, and being very much interested in the story, she used to get quite vexed that Barbara could not find more time for reading.

Thus it happened one morning, when Barbara came up stairs after breakfast to make the beds, Helen said,

"I'll make the beds, Barbara, you sit down and read another chapter, so that you can tell it to me before school time."

"Oh no, I cannot; mother always wishes us to do our own work."

"To be sure she does, as a general thing, but she would not care for once."

"I'm afraid she would," said Barbara, at the same time casting a longing look at the book on the table.

"How foolish you are, Barbara, standing there; you might have had a chapter half read by this time. I think Mrs. Neville would laugh at the idea of objecting to my making the beds once for you," and Helen began spreading the bed-clothes.

Barbara, after a little hesitation took up the book, saying to herself, "Doing it only this one morning cannot make much difference." Helen finished the work, and then listened to the chapter with delighted interest. But Barbara did not feel at all comfortable. Nevertheless, the next morning when Helen, without saying anything, began making the beds, Barbara, not feeling quite so badly as she did the day before, read another chapter. Ah, when once we give way to the *first* temptation, how hard it is to resist the others! Nothing else that Helen could have offered, would have tempted Barbara so much, as an opportunity to read. Barbara would at any time rather read than play. And this was Helen's boasted improvement! She was not only sinning herself but coaxing another to sin. For disobedience, even in

I

the slightest thing, is breaking God's holy commandment.

"Where have you been so long, this morning, Helen?" asked Mrs. Neville, "you have nothing to do up stairs to-day; I have been waiting for you. I wish you would please take this pitcher, and bring me some molasses from the store."

Helen did not answer; a burning blush spread over her face.

"Mother," said Nora, noticing Helen's reluctance, "Helen has never been to the store; let her wipe these plates, and I will go."

"I know she has never been," replied her mother, "and so I want her to go, and learn the way; for some time, you and Barbara might not be here."

Still Helen did not move, and Mrs. Neville, who was standing with her back towards her, turned round to look at her. When she saw the young girl's face, she said,

"Why, what is the matter, Helen?"

"I do not want to go after molasses."

"Why not?" asked Mrs. Neville with evident surprise.

"Because,"—said Helen, stopping short.

"Because is no reason, Helen, why do you not wish to go?"

"At home we kept a servant to run errands," answered Helen, proudly.

Mrs. Neville looked at her; and there was so much sorrow and compassion in the gaze, that Helen reddened beneath it, and heartily wished she had said nothing.

"Do you think, Helen, there is anything disgraceful in bringing molasses from the store?" she asked, at length.

Helen looked down, and did not answer.

"Poor foolish child!" continued Mrs. Neville, "you have been imbibing very proud and sinful notions. It is said that once, when Washington was commander-in-chief, a corporal in his army refused to help his men throw up fortifications. He was too *proud* to do it, because he was a *corporal*. Washington hearing of it went to the spot and commenced helping the soldiers, working as hard as any of them, until the young corporal, filled with shame, gladly took his share of the work. Had you been there, Helen, which part would you have acted? Ah, Helen, my child, God give you grace to conquer that foolish pride We never read in the Bible of the Saviour's pride, although he was Lord of all. No, his earthly life was spent among earth's poorest ones, ministering to their wants. Pray to him for some portion of his lovely humility."

Helen without saying anything, took down her hat, and went out. She was touched by Mrs. Neville's kindness and forbearance, and ashamed of her own conduct. As she walked through the shady lane, she made up her mind that she would never be so foolish again; and that, no matter what she had to do, she would do it with pleasure. She walked along, thinking thus, until she was quite persuaded that she had cured herself already. But, alas, for the keeping of such hastily made resolutions! Helen had not gone far, when whom should she see approaching but Mary Rellim? Mary was dressed very prettily, and a delicate little sunshade was in her hand. In an instant all Helen's brave resolutions were over. Mary Rellim had told her that she would have to run errands, and work; and even if it were true, Helen made up her mind that Mary should not know it. What to do with the pitcher was Helen's first thought. There was no time to hide it; Mary might look up any moment, and see her. A field, with a low fence, lay on one side of her, so she dropped the pitcher over as gently as possible, and then sat down to wait Mary's coming, trying to think how she should account for her presence there, at that time of the morning. But Helen was spared the sin of that deceit, for Mary turned down another road, without seeing her. Helen looked after her with all her former longings. She wished for a hat and feather, and a silk dress, just like those; and with all her old reluctance she turned to find the pitcher. Once over the fence she saw it, but in picking it up only the handle came up in her hand—the pitcher was broken! Helen's first thought was one of pleasure that she could not go to the store; her next was, what *would* Mrs. Neville say? But Helen had been brought up in too free and careless a manner to have much fear about her; when, therefore, she entered the kitchen, she answered at once to Mrs. Neville's look of surprise,

"I broke the pitcher."

"How did you come to break it?" asked Mrs. Neville.

"I threw it down," answered Helen, coloring.

12

"Threw it down!" repeated Mrs. Neville, " why, what did you do that for?"

But to this question Helen returned no answer. Mrs. Neville asked again and again. But Helen would not tell. She was ashamed of it herself, and that was bad enough to bear; she would not give them the opportunity of thinking her so silly. Mrs. Neville said kindly, but firmly,

"Helen, I cannot allow disobedience and stubbornness. Go to your room, and do not leave it until you have made up your mind to tell me the whole truth."

Helen turned with flashing eyes to resist this order; but there was firmness in Mrs. Neville's face, with all its gentleness, which seemed to say, "I *will* be obeyed," and Helen left the room.

Into the balmy breath of the summer air, as it came in at the open window, Helen carried the gloom of her own sinful heart. She threw herself on the floor, and yielded to a burst of tears. This was the first time in her life that she had ever been punished, and with all the might of her haughty spirit she rebelled against it.

"What right has Mrs. Neville to punish me? I am not her own daughter. I was beginning to

love her; now I do not like her at all. To try
and *make* me answer her question, as if I were a
little child! I never will tell, *never!* She may keep
me here as long as she pleases. No, she cannot
keep me here if I do not choose to stay; and I
will not stay long Why should I do what I
never had to do at home? Ah, there I was
happy. Margaret loved me, and she never made
me mind. At Mrs. Rellim's, too, I was happy.
Why did I come here, where I am so miserable?
I have never been happy here, never!"

That was partly true. From the time she had
first come to live at Mrs. Neville's, she had not been
happy. For she was constantly reminded by the
lives of those around her that she was treading in
the wrong path. It broke in upon her self-com-
placency, and made her discontented. Then she
had striven to imitate them, and that only added
to her vexation, because she always failed. Pride
kept her from seeking counsel of Mrs. Neville,
and thus those six weeks had passed away, and been
the most unhappy of her life. The young dislike
to suffer. They turn from the bitter cup with
loathing. But God knows always what is best.
The Holy Spirit was striving with her, trying to

win her to a Saviour's love; but still she refused.
"All deep joy is born of sorrow." Would Helen
one day step from the deep sorrow of repentance
to the sweet joy of sins forgiven through a Saviour's love and mercy?

The morning hours passed slowly. She thought
of the pleasant little study. It was the morning
for the French lesson, and she would not be there
to laugh at Nora's efforts at pronunciation. Then
she wondered if they missed her, and a wish came
that she could begin the morning over again,
and act differently; banished instantly by the
thought that it could not be helped now, and she
would not give up.

Alas! for misimproved time! How many of us
can look back and long for the return of wasted
years, that we might live them better. But time
sweeps by as rapidly as though its hours did not
mould the immortal life of man. The days have
been, and they are not, and they return no more.
God grant that no one who reads this narrative,
may look back from a dying bed, with a wild
longing to recall the years in which he never
thought of God, or prepared to meet him!

Mrs. Neville brought Helen's dinner up, and

asked, kindly, if she was ready to talk with her; but Helen merely answered, "No, ma'am," and refused to taste anything, and Mrs. Neville went down again, much disappointed.

The day seemed very long to Helen; and it was very long to Barbara and Nora also. When play-time came, nothing interested them, and Barbara sat down to read, wishing she could go and tell Helen the different interesting things as she came to them. Nora begged several times to go up and coax Helen, but Mrs. Neville would not allow it. The evening was very quiet. Mrs. Neville had gone up with Helen's supper, and returned with the same result.

When Nora and Barbara went to bed, they listened, but all was quiet in the next room; for Helen had gone to sleep early. The two girls talked a little about her, and hoped that by to-morrow all would be right. Nora whispered a soft good night at Helen's door, jumped into bed, and was soon fast asleep. Barbara read her Bible, and was just going to blow out the candle, when her eye lighted on Robinson Crusoe. She had been reading part of an interesting chapter, and thought she would just finish it before she retired. But

12*

when that was completed, she must see how the next chapter began. While thus reading she soon forgot everything around her; and when her mother closed a shutter down stairs, preparatory to going to bed, Barbara started as though some one had struck her. She hastily put out the light and jumped into bed, without saying her prayers. When once in bed, she trembled so, she could think of nothing for some time. Barbara knew that her mother never allowed them to sit up at night, and she wondered how she could have disobeyed so easily. She forgot that one little act of deceit opens the door to many larger ones. She had deceived in allowing Helen to do her work, while she read, and having read several times at forbidden hours, it was no wonder that her greatest failing easily conquered her, instead of her conquering it. Barbara could not sleep. She tossed restlessly about. She heard her mother go to bed, and then all was quiet. Barbara had not felt very comfortable the last few days; she had been acting wrongly, and so her prayers had not been sincere. Her conscience troubled her, and she tried to put it off by promising never to do so again. At last, wearied out, she fell into a troubled slumber.

X.

REPENTANCE.

" With tears of anguish I lament,
  Here at thy feet, my God,
  My passion, pride, and discontent,
  And vile ingratitude."

IT has always seemed a strange thing to me that
people should call daily life tame and monotonous. While the soul wages a constant warfare
with the evil around it, while it struggles onward
and upward towards a higher existence, while the
heart with all its warm affections, is sometimes led
astray, even by its most generous impulses, while
the mind, with all its heaven endowed intellect
can read everywhere the vastness and glory of
creation, while life is filled with deep sorrow and
agonizing conflicts, and blessed with the sweet
touch of joy,—there must be, even in the life of the
most humble, thoughts, feelings, and struggles,
enough to make one day entirely different from
another. Day after day, no matter what our out-

139

ward life may be, the soul-life changes. Through the petty cares of one day we step at eventide one pace nearer Christian perfection, or one pace farther off. No standing still is possible to the immortal, fighting each step of his way towards the promised crown. In the face of such a thought, how can daily life become monotonous? It assumes a fearful responsibility that should snatch from it every feeling of ennui or careless indifference, that should make us long to improve each hour. For hours are the little rivulets that are bearing us on to the river of death, to be swept out into the great ocean of eternity.

It was a day of clouded sunshine to both Barbara and Helen. They awoke with the impression that something had gone wrong. Barbara's head ached, and she felt altogether out of sorts. Mrs. Neville inquired, almost as soon as they came down stairs, if the light was burning in their room when she closed the shutters; and Nora hastened at once to assure her that it could not have been, as they undressed themselves and made ready for bed at once. Barbara was on the point of confessing, but she checked herself when she remembered that very probably her mother, as a punishment, would not let her finish the book. This decided her. She could not bear the idea of giving up the story without knowing how it ended. But poor Barbara spent a miserable morning. When her mother at family worship prayed so earnestly for the sinful Helen, Barbara thought she must tell at once, and not act a falsehood any longer. After breakfast she looked so miserable, and her head really ached so badly, that her mother sent her up stairs to lie down. Nora darkened the room, and brought the cologne; and was so pitiful and kind that Barbara could hardly bear it.

As for Helen, nothing like sorrow filled her heart. Her anger and indignation only increased. From thinking her lot hard, she had come to believe it the worst that possibly could be, and herself the most ill-treated girl. She looked out at the bright sunshine; and the song of birds, the lowing of cattle, the drowsy insect hum, the rustling leaves, and murmuring brooks, all seemed to be calling her to come forth. It was a hard punishment to have to stay in the house such a lovely day. Helen determined that she would endure it no longer. She had heard the clock strike nine, and she knew they must all be in the study; so opening and closing her door gently, and slipping quietly down stairs, she ran off into the woods. When once there, she thought she would enjoy herself. She believed that the reason she had felt so badly was because she was shut up in one room; but she soon found that all the beauty of nature had no power to "minister to a mind diseased." She walked round to find something amusing, but nothing pleased her; and throwing herself down on the ground she gave herself up to the thoughts she could not banish. One thing she made up her mind to, as she was idly pulling a flower to pieces,—that she would not go back to Mrs. Neville's.

"No," said Helen, speaking to herself, as she was in the habit of doing, "why should I go back there, to be scolded and punished, and worried all the time about religion, and frightened about dying? Dying! When I am only fourteen, and Old Dugald said 'my cheek was like the summer's rose!' Mr. Ashton used to say, 'God orders all things,' and Mrs. Neville has told me many times, that God must have taken me from Mrs. Rellim's for some wise purpose. But I will not believe it. If God is a God of love, as they say he is, he would not give us trouble and sorrow. I will go back to Mrs. Rellim's, and stay until my father sends for me. She told me to stay months, if I wished, and I was foolish to leave so soon. It cannot be long before I once more go home,—home to dear Scotland. By her bonny braes I may linger the day long with none to chide."

Thus Helen's thoughts ran on, and an hour passed in idle dreaming, when she was roused by hasty footsteps, and saw John Rellim coming towards her. Helen got up quickly, and put herself on her guard against any of his mischief. But no fun sparkled in John's eye; he merely said, "Good morning," and was hastening on, when Helen stopped him with the question,

"What are you in such a hurry for, John?"

John turned towards her for a minute, and Helen was startled to see how pale he was, and to notice the tears in his eyes. He did not seem at all like mischievous John Rellim, as he said,

"O Helen, I'm going for the doctor. All the children have the diphtheria, and Gussie died this morning," and John ran on without waiting for her sympathy; and indeed Helen would have given him none. Never in her life had she received such a shock; and coming at such a time, when anger and pride and rebellion were reigning in her heart! She had laughed at the idea of dying, because she was so young and healthy; and there, at that moment, death had taken one younger, and full as blooming as she. She had said in all the pride of her heart, that she would go back to that house from which God had seen best to take her. Struck with a remorse which could not find vent in words, she threw herself on the ground, with a passionate cry for forgiveness. To Helen, in her overwrought state, it seemed as though God had purposely taken her away to save her, and she had been resisting with all her power his tender love and care. Oh, how weak, and pitiful, and unworthy seemed her anger and pride now, in the presence of death.

What matter where we live, or how, if death find us ready for the Master's call? In order fully to appreciate Helen's feelings, we must remember the state of mind she had been in. She had thought to be, and to do, everything good by her own efforts, and failing in this, she had defiantly said to herself that to the lot that was given her she would never submit. She had determined to brave all things. Even when told that God's hand would guide, she had refused that guidance. And it seemed to her in those frightful moments as she lay there on the ground, that God would do well to strike her dead also. She had refused the winning counsels of his pure religion; she had resisted the influence of his Holy Spirit; and yet he had not given her up, but had sent a thrilling warning to meet her in all her wilfulness and pride. She wept with a sorrow as wild as her gratitude was deep. The life of the last few weeks passed before her, stained with its self-righteousness, anger, and neglected duty; and Helen felt humbled to the very dust. She remembered Mrs. Neville's earnest prayers that they might be a united Christian family, having one faith, one Saviour; and how she, in secret, had resented thus being prayed about! Ah, she remembered everything but too keenly, down to that very morning when she had left her home in anger and stubbornness, determined to return no more. Her heart yearned for reconciliation. She longed to hear Mrs. Neville's voice whisper peace and com-

13   K

fort. Helen never did anything by halves. If her stubbornness and anger had been deep and lasting, so also was her repentance. She determined to go back at once and confess all.

Nora had begun her lessons that morning, but her mind was so evidently distracted between Barbara's illness and Helen's punishment, that Mrs. Neville soon closed the book, and told her to bring her sewing.

They sat quietly sewing in the study; neither had spoken for some time, for Mrs. Neville was anxious and worried about Helen, and meditating some new way of winning her over. The afternoon before, she had spent much time in earnest prayer for this wandering girl; and then she had gone to her and striven to show her her sin, and the love and mercy of her Saviour. She had prayed with her, but Helen only seemed to grow more hardened; and this morning Mrs. Neville's heart failed her. She had gone for strength and guidance to the only source whence they can come, but notwithstanding this she felt sad and disappointed. She knew the fearful responsibility of training up a girl of Helen's disposition, and she longed to see her safe in the arms of a true faith—one of Christ's lambs.

As the door opened and Helen entered, Mrs. Neville, supposing her to have just come from her own room, almost started with joy. She had been desponding, and God had reproved her thus. Helen entered the room with a slow step and downcast eye; but when she got near Mrs. Neville, she threw herself on her knees, and clasping her round the waist, she exclaimed,

"Oh, forgive me, forgive me! I have been so wicked," and then bursting into tears, she laid her head in her kind friend's lap.

"Dear Helen," said Mrs. Neville, putting her hand on the young girl's bowed head, "we all err, and go astray like lost sheep. Thankful should we be when our Father shows us our error, and leads us through the path of repentance to lasting peace."

"Oh, you do not know how wicked I have been; I ran away this morning!"

Mrs. Neville could not repress a slight start on hearing this, and Nora rose to leave the room.

"Do not go, Nora," said Helen sadly, "I wish you to know just how wicked I have been. I feel as though it would do me good to tell every one of my foolish pride."

Nora sat down very reluctantly. It pained her to hear Helen's confession; for Nora was apt to place those she loved on a pinnacle of goodness, and refused to believe in her own heart that they could go wrong. Helen was so pretty, so lively, so kind, that Nora had considered her almost perfect, and had welcomed her admission to the family with unbounded joy. But day after day Nora had been obliged to make excuses to herself for Helen's conduct, and both she and Barbara had found that everything was not so delightful as they had anticipated. But this was the crowning point of Nora's sorrow, that Helen should act so stubbornly towards their darling mother; and she longed to escape without hearing all the sad story. But as this was impossible, she took her seat once more, and her tears mingled with Helen's, as the sorrowful confession was made.

Helen told all unreservedly, with many a deep blush and irrepressible sob, from the breaking of the pitcher, to the meeting of John Rellim in the woods. Helen's character had this redeeming trait, that when once convinced of wrong, she never sought to excuse, or palliate her fault, but blamed and reproached herself even more than others did. Mrs. Neville understood better than Helen could tell her, how the shock of Augusta's death, meeting her as it did while filled with rebellious feelings towards God, had showed Helen her sins in such a startling light that it made her almost despair. But in all this Mrs. Neville recognized the hand of God. It pleases him to allow some of his lambs to go through green pastures into the sweet valley of eternal peace; but others must first bruise themselves among the sharp rocks of sorrow, or be almost lost in the quicksands of worldliness and pride, ere they are caught up into the arms of Divine love, and sheltered safe from all harm in the fold of a Saviour's bosom.

Very gently Mrs. Neville talked to the young girl. She assured her of her forgiveness, and then besought her to turn for pardon and peace to the Saviour. But to all Mrs. Neville's entreaties, Helen had but one cry,

"Oh, dear Mrs. Neville, you do not know how wicked I have been, not only *now*, but *always*. How can I ask Jesus to forgive me, and save me,

13 *

when only this morning I said I did not love him, and I would not try to do right."

"Ah, well then, Helen," said Mrs. Neville sadly, "I am to understand that you never intend to come to the Saviour. You always wish to live on in this way, without his love and help."

"Oh, no, ma'am," answered Helen, very much startled, "I do indeed long to be a Christian, I will go to him as soon as I have learned to behave better."

"My dear girl, you will never learn to behave better, without his help. Human nature, unassisted by the Divine, must always stray from the narrow path. You remember Jesus said, 'I came not to call the righteous, but sinners to repentance.' If you could learn to be good yourself, what would be the use of a Saviour? Just as you are, dear Helen, go to him, tell him all your sins, confess all your wicked thoughts, ask him to have mercy on you, and to forgive you, to teach you daily and hourly how best to govern yourself, and to love and serve him. Will you do it, Helen, dear?"

Helen looked up eagerly, into Mrs. Neville's face.

"Are you *sure;* are you *quite sure,* he will hear and forgive?" she asked passionately.

"I am sure," answered Mrs. Neville solemnly. "Do you think, Helen, when the Saviour was willing to come here to earth, and die on the cruel cross; willing to suffer and bear all he did, on purpose to save you; do you think when he finds you turning to him with a prayer to be forgiven and saved, that he will turn you away? Why, my child, if he did not wish you to live with him forever in glory, why did he come here and die? No, Helen; *such* love could never turn away from a supplicant."

"No, never," said the girl; "I believe it, I believe it. Pray for me."

Mrs. Neville prayed, and when the prayer was finished, Helen rose, and quietly kissing Mrs. Neville and Nora, went up to her own room. Very different were her feelings on entering it, from the rebellious ones with which she had left it. Now Helen knelt by the little bed and breathed forth her first *real* prayer,—a confession of sins, a cry for forgiveness, and an earnest asking for God's Holy Spirit to guide and direct her. This was the beginning of Helen's Christian life.

With many a tearful struggle, many a slippery footstep, she trod onward in the narrow way; but she felt there was ever a Saviour's hand to guide and help, ever a divine compassion to forgive. And if, in after years, she learned to walk with a surer step, and firmer faith, she still looked back with grateful thankfulness to the hours of sorrow in Brookfield, which were the starting point in her Christian career.

Helen did not leave her room that day, except to eat her dinner; she wished to stay alone and think. Mrs. Neville went at once to Mrs. Rellim's to offer her services. Animosities die under the hand of deep sorrow. Mrs. Rellim gladly accepted Mrs. Neville's aid, and she did not come home until late. Barbara's head still ached; and Nora felt disconsolate as she wandered around the empty house. She could not go to Helen, and she did not like to disturb Barbara. She read a little while, but Nora was not much of a reader. and she soon laid down the book to think of little Gussie, who was lying so cold and still in the stately bed chamber.

After a while Nora put on the tea kettle, toasted a nice slice of toast, and took it, with a cup of tea, up to Barbara. But Barbara refused to eat, and Nora thought she would not trouble her by telling her of Gussie's death, as she had intended to do.

Nora then got supper ready, and called Helen, and they ate alone, as Mrs. Neville had told them not to wait for her. At any other time it would have been grand fun for Helen and Nora to eat alone, and for Nora to sit at the head of the table and pour out; but now they both felt too sad to give anything more than a passing smile. Helen inquired where Barbara was; and then the conversation turned on the loving qualities of the dead child. Helen after supper helped Nora wash the dishes, and they both sat down on the porch to watch the glowing sunset, and to await Mrs. Neville's return; talking in sweet, girlish voices of life's responsibilities, of death's dark shadow, and of the bright life beyond, Nora's fervent faith whispering the sublime promises of the Bible to cheer the timid heart of her companion.

Thus they sat, twined in each other's arms, until the stars came out and looked down on that picture of bright, youthful loveliness—a picture of beautiful young life dedicating its freshest, purest possessions and powers to the service of its Maker.

XI.

BARBARA'S CONFESSION.

"I bar thee not from faults:
    God wot it were in vain!
Inalienable heritage
    Since that primeval stain!
The wisest have been fools,
    The surest stumbled sore,
Strive thou to stand—or fall'n to rise,
    I ask thee not for more!"

THE next morning school duties recommenced as usual. No, not quite as usual; for Helen, although feeling happier than she had done for some time, could not shake off the idea of the responsibility of life which she had realized the day before for the first time. She had prayed that morning for strength and guidance, but the memory of a recent sorrow still left her smile sad and her spirit pained. Barbara said her head was better, but she looked so pale, and looked so little like her usual self, that Mrs. Neville was quite troubled; but Barbara insisted so urgently on doing her work and learning her lessons, that Mrs. Neville consented.

Poor Barbara wished to forget her wrong doing. Unaccustomed to conceal the truth in the slightest thing, the deception she had practiced about the book worried her almost beyond endurance. But she could not make up her mind to confess. Nora had always such a habit of saying, "Oh, Barbara dear, I wish I was like you, you never do anything wrong," that Barbara now could not bear the idea of Nora's knowing how she had acted. And then, too, her mother must know it, and Helen. Barbara's thoughts were ever on the subject, whether she had before her a geography or an arithmetic, and she made so many mistakes in her music lesson, that Mrs. Neville kindly closed the piano and told her to wait until to-morrow.

Thus passed the morning. As soon as dinner was over Mrs. Neville went to Mrs. Rellim's and left the girls during the study and sewing hours. When playtime came, at four o'clock, Barbara went and lay down on the lounge in the dining-room. Nora and Helen agreed not to go out, but to sit there and keep her company.

"Dear sister," said Nora, leaning fondly over

the end of the lounge, "I am so sorry you cannot come out and play and enjoy yourself."

"Don't worry me, Nora," said Barbara, pushing away Nora's hand from her head.

"No, I won't," said Nora, leaving the lounge; "does talking trouble you, sister?"

"No."

Nora looked quite relieved. She tried to think of something pleasant to say; and knowing Barbara's love of books, she asked,

"How do you like Robinson Crusoe?"

She could not have hit on a more disagreeable subject. Barbara answered peevishly,

"Do stop asking me that every few minutes, Nora?"

Nora looked surprised.

"I only meant it kindly. How your head must ache to make you speak so. Mother says I may read it when you have finished it, if I don't blot my copy book for two weeks."

Barbara made no reply, and Helen just then coming into the room, she turned towards her, and said,

"I wish, Helen, you would take a walk in the garden with me."

"Yes, Barbara, if you wish it," said Helen, looking surprised. They went out, and Nora, laying her head on the lounge, cried quietly. Barbara had preferred Helen to her. While Nora was thus mourning over her sister's strange coolness, Barbara had determined to confide in Helen. She knew nothing of yesterday's proceedings; but she knew that Helen must have confessed, or she would not have been out of her room. Helen had not spoken of her influencing Barbara to read instead of first finishing her work, for she did not wish to involve Barbara, but it had worried her a great deal all the morning, and she suspected that that was in reality what ailed Barbara. She did not like to mention the subject first, and they walked almost to the end of the garden before Barbara spoke.

"Helen, I am very unhappy, I disobeyed mother so about that book; and I have kept it secret so long."

"It was all my fault, Barbara. I have been worried about it all this morning. I was going to ask you to let me tell."

Barbara looked astonished. She had expected Helen would try and persuade her that she had

14

done nothing wrong, and although she knew it would not be true, yet still it would be some consolation to hear it. Helen noticed her look, and said sadly,

"I don't wonder you look surprised to hear me give such advice; but oh, Barbara, my eyes were first opened yesterday to regard my conduct in its true light, as very sinful and hateful in God's sight. Ah, if he will only help me, I will try and lead a better life. I say, *if;* I *know* he will help me. I felt it this morning when I said my prayers."

Barbara was much surprised; and not only surprised, but pleased, for although she had yielded to temptation, she was in heart a Christian, and she rejoiced to think that Helen was trying to walk in the true path. She put her arms around her, and fondly kissing her, said,

"I am very glad to hear it, dear Helen; now we are all three sisters indeed."

"Sisters forever," said Helen, returning the embrace, "and now, Barbara, tell your mother everything, when she comes home to night. Do, please, promise."

Barbara stood irresolute.

"Never mind," said Helen, generously, "I will tell."

"Oh, no, no, I must do it; mother would be still more sorry to find me such a coward."

"You will do it then, Barbara, my sister, will you not?" said Helen coaxingly. Barbara promised that she would.

Let none of my readers be surprised that Helen should, on the first occasion, act with a conscientiousness and openness, which bespoke a long practice in Christian warfare, instead of the experience of a few hours. It is very seldom that the young disciple yields to the first temptation. In the first glow of love and hope, we are strong. It is when weeks have passed away, and something of our first ardor has abated, that we become less watchful, and fall into sin. Besides, the memory of her own unhappiness was too fresh in Helen's mind not to make her wish to guard another against it. Then, too, Helen wished to confess her own share in Barbara's unhappy fall. As I have said before, she never did anything by halves. Deep and true had been her repentance, and she therefore wished to confess all. Helen knew that her faults were not conquered, that they were only sleeping. She knew that they must be met and subdued by the help of her Saviour, day by day, as temptation revealed them. Yet she longed now, at once, to do all in her power; and she felt that all would not be done until she had told of her deceitfulness.

"How lonely Nora must be," said Helen, after they had talked a while longer, "shall I call her?"

"No, I'll go call her. Poor child, I wonder how I could have spoken so crossly to her."

"There she is," said Helen; and they both went towards her. Nora stooped very low over a lovely white rose, that they might not see the traces of tears on her face.

"Is it not beautiful?" she asked, as they came up, "I am going to take these two buds to-morrow, to lay in Gussie's coffin."

"Most lovely," said Helen, stooping down to smell it.

Barbara stooped also, but it was to kiss Nora's rosy cheek. Nora looked around smiling.

"Yes," said Barbara, "I am trying to kiss away the memory of those cross words I said."

"Never mind," said Nora, returning the kiss,

"Oh, Helen! how could you get up there."   p. 178.

"you had a headache, and that sometimes puts one out of humor."

"No, no, it was not that, Nora; I have been acting very wrongly, and it has worried me, and made me cross."

"It was my fault," interrupted Helen, and she narrated the circumstances, generously trying to shield Barbara; but Nora could not help looking shocked when she heard that her sister had actually sat up that night, and kept the lamp burning. This was a great trial to Barbara, but it gave her, what she had not had before, a clear idea of how deeply she had sinned, and how guilty she must appear in the sight of God; and leaving her young companions abruptly she went up to her own room to ask with truly penitent tears, for forgiveness and for strength to do better. But if Barbara felt badly then, she felt much worse when she saw her mother's grieved and surprised look. Indeed Mrs. Neville could scarcely believe that Barbara would act so, she had always trusted her so fully. Then, in words which Barbara felt she could never forget, Mrs. Neville pointed out to her the danger of yielding to the first little omission of duty.

14 *   L

"And to think, my daughter," she continued, "of the dreadful responsibility of your influence. You have come out before the world as the Lord's child; you have promised to follow in the Saviour's footsteps, and to do all in your power to forward his cause; and yet, look at the stumbling-block you were placing in Helen's way. What do you suppose Helen must have thought of a religion whose professors were influenced so easily to go astray? How could you have hoped to win Helen to Christ, after first leading her to practice deceit?"

"Indeed, mother, I never thought of it in that dreadful light."

"I believe you did not, my child; but you must remember, when you do wrong, you can never tell how far the influence of that wrong extends. It is a fearful thought that perhaps some slight fault of ours may keep another from seeking Christ."

With these solemn words, Mrs. Neville left her. Barbara had never before in her life, felt as she then did the great responsibility of being a Christian. She saw, for the first time, that the honor of the church and the glorifying of Christ, were entrusted to each Christian; that as he behaves, the world will judge of the Master he professes to follow. Oh, if any of my young readers have taken upon themselves the sacred name of Christian, if they have come out before the world and promised to be on the Lord's side, let them pause here, and ask themselves the solemn question, "Am I honoring the cause of Christ? Will those around me learn to love religion, from seeing the way it influences my life? Do I show, by each daily word, and act, that Christ is to me above all else?" If you cannot answer these questions satisfactorily, then stop, and begin anew. Ask help of Jesus, that your life may grow into a more perfect Christian life, that others "may see your good works, and glorify your Father which is in heaven."

The next day the funeral took place. Very calm and sweet the little face looked lying on its last pillow. Nora laid the white rose buds gently on the waxen hand, and Helen sobbed aloud. Gussie had been so kind to her in the short time she had been with her, that she had learned to love her. Helen remembered, too, that Gussie was the only one who had regretted parting with her.

No one stood at the grave but the stricken mother and a few friends, for Mr. Rellim was a sea captain, and not at home, and the children were all sick. How did Mrs. Rellim feel? God alone knew in that solemn hour, whether she heeded the warning. To a mother, giving her child back to him who gave it, it is a bitter trial, even when a Saviour's pitying love comforts and assures the bereaved one of a blest reunion. But to a mother standing at the grave of her little one with no faith in God, no hope of a future bliss, no comfort in a Saviour's tenderness, wild and bitter indeed must be that parting. To the sublime promises that form such a precious part of the burial service, Mrs. Rellim could not listen, and she turned from the grave with a shudder, to go home and strive with all of human power to save her other children. And if they were saved, would she so bring them up that they might one day go and meet their sister?

God pity the mother whose darlings he takes to heaven, while she stands far away and looks up with straining eyes towards their bright home, in which she has no share!

XII.

MR. NELSON'S FARM.

"Play on, play on, I am with you there,
In the midst of your merry ring;
I can feel the thrill of the daring jump,
And the rush of the breathless swing.
I hide with you in the fragrant hay,
And I whoop the smothered call,
And my feet slip up on the seedy floor,
And I care not for the fall."

SEVERAL weeks had gone by, and things were wearing a cheerful aspect in the cottage. It was August, and that month was always a holiday month at Mrs. Neville's, as she considered it too warm to keep the children in the school-room. Those weeks had brought many trials for Helen. Her eye would flash with anger at a slight reproof, or she would indolently waste her time; and only gradually was she learning that Christianity must mould one's every day life. No answer had been received to Mrs. Neville's letter, and she had writ-

165

ten another, although Helen's longing wish to go home was fast vanishing.

One morning while Nora and Barbara were dressing, Helen ran into the room exclaiming,

"Oh, girls, I have been thinking of such a splendid thing,—a pic-nic!"

"A pic-nic?" they both said at once.

"Yes, why not?" said Helen, "we could take our dinners, and go to the woods, and stay all day."

"Oh, that would be splendid," said Nora, clapping her hands, "but who all would go?"

"Why our sewing circle, of course."

"I think mother would not object," said Barbara.

"No indeed," answered Helen, as having finished dressing, she sat down on the bed; "just think of staying all day, and eating our dinners off the ground."

"I hope the ground will be cleaner than usual," said Barbara, laughing.

"Well now, Barbara," said Helen, joining in the laugh, "you ought not to run down the ground that way, for you would be in a pretty fix without it."

"I'm afraid she would," said Nora, "but I think we'll be in a hungry fix after a while, if we don't get breakfast."

"Oh, sure enough," said Helen, "I really don't believe the table will set itself if I stay here. Ah, Nora, as they say in Scotland, 'ye have the lang head,'" and Helen ran down stairs, and set the table with so many extra flourishes of fun that Mrs. Neville was induced to inquire what was the matter. Then out came the account of the pic-nic, in which Nora and Barbara joined when they came down. Mrs. Neville said she had no objections, but that the arrangements could not be made in a day, as the children seemed to think. Unexpected help, however, came in to favor the girls.

Mr. Nelson, Mrs. Neville's landlord, was a frequent visitor at the cottage. Many people wondered what attraction drew the polished, wealthy bachelor to that unpretending home. It was—although Mr. Nelson would not have acknowledged it to himself—the charm of true piety. Mr. Nelson had been unfortunate in his dealings with his fellow-men, and because he had met with some bearing the name of Christian who did not act up to the high principles they professed, he made light of religion and its professors. He had tried the world, but the upright honor and the pure morality he expected to find, he did not, and he turned from all mankind with something of a misanthrope's feelings. Much of this was owing to the manner in which he had been educated. His father, made a widower by the birth of this only child, had brought him up to an almost purely intellectual life. Howard Nelson's world had been his books. From the heroes of antiquity, from the wild chivalry of the middle ages, he had at his father's death stepped out into real life, when he was twenty-five, expecting to find men the realization of what history paints them. It was no wonder, then, that he was a disappointed man. The only firm principles, the only pure, unsullied faith to be found on earth he rejected when he refused the religion of Christ. He gave up society, and settled in Brookfield. Here he once met little Nora Neville. Her gay, frank, yet modest manners pleased him; and finding that she was the daughter of an old friend, and lived in one of his cottages, with the strange whims that we sometimes take, he called at the house. No; I do wrong to call it a whim. God alone knows how often he causes these seeming chances to work us some eternal good. All that Mr. Nelson saw in his frequent visits, led him to recognize the pure faith and true piety of which he had fondly dreamed, yet never before had realized. This was the charm, though unconfessed, that drew him so often to the pretty cottage.

Helen, with Nora's large apron on, was kneeling in the yard, scouring the knives, as Mr. Nelson came up the gravel path, and walked round to the kitchen door with the familiarity of an old friend. Helen had never seen him before, for he had been for some time absent from home on business. Mr. Nelson looked at her with some surprise, and when he went in inquired who she was. He had come up to invite Barbara and Nora to go and spend the next day at his farm, about half a mile below Brookfield; now, of course, he included Helen also. He only staid a few minutes, setting an early hour the next morning to call for them.

The girls were almost wild with delight; Nora ran out to tell Helen, and rolled her over and over in the grass until she cried out for her to stop.

"It will just do instead of our pic-nic," said Helen.

15

"Oh, a great deal better, Helen, for he has such a splendid place, and so many fine things."

The rest of the day seemed to pass very slowly, even to Barbara, who could usually console herself for any delay with a nice book. But all days must come to an end; and the girls very readily acquiesced in Mrs. Neville's proposal that they should retire half an hour earlier than usual, to prepare for the extra exertion of the morrow. And when the morrow came, three pairs of eyes glanced eagerly out of the window, as soon as they were open. Yes, there was the sun just beginning to rise above the horizon. In a few seconds he came up with a splendor that quite satisfied even youthful expectations.

Everything was still bathed in the lovely freshness of morning, as the carriage rolled away from the door, and the girls kissed their hands in a merry good-bye to Mrs. Neville. To be sure, the distance was not great; they could easily have walked it; but Mr. Nelson was bent on giving them as much pleasure as possible; therefore he called in his carriage, and they drove round two or three miles, before they brought up at the farmhouse. This was a large stone building with barns, out-houses, pig-pens, a splendid dairy, and spring-house. Mr. Nelson understood well how to please young folks; so, soon as the girls alighted, he said,

"Now, scamper; there is the barn to hunt eggs in, and down there is the spring-house, and beyond is the woods. Just run wild; but when you hear the dinner horn, come back here to the house."

No second bidding was needed. They certainly did run wild. The great barn re-echoed their racing footsteps, and the deep woods their laughter. They took off their shoes and stockings, and waded ankle deep in the little brook. They picked the wild flowers, and chased the butterflies; and when at twelve o'clock the dinner horn sounded, they could scarcely believe it possible that the day was so far advanced. But when they got back to the house, a pleasant surprise awaited them. Mr. Nelson's own house and grounds adjoined his farm. They had passed it coming down, but it stood so far back from the road, and was so shut in by trees, that Helen had not noticed it. A servant conducted them to the end of the farm grounds, and opening a small gate, they entered what seemed to them almost a fairy scene. Here were woods so beautifully laid out and so dense, that as they entered it appeared like the approach of twilight, instead of noontide. Through the centre ran a small stream, with many a tiny cataract, and spanned by rustic bridges.

"How delightful! How lovely!" exclaimed Nora and Barbara. But Helen said nothing. Almost breathless, she was looking at the beauty around her. Her love of nature was too deep, her appreciation too keen, for words. And there, in this cool, lovely place, they were to dine. Here was spread a round table just for the three; and the exercise of the morning was not calculated to diminish their enjoyment of the chicken, custards, peaches, and iced milk set before them. The meal was certainly well digested if laughing has any-thing to do with it; for they were so upside down with the novelty of waiting on themselves, and of being the only ones at the table, that Nora helped Helen twice to potatoes, before she began to eat, and Helen put a spoonful of gravy in Bar-bara's tumbler of milk, and so Barbara was obliged to drink out of Nora's glass.

When dinner was over Mr. Nelson made his

appearance, and they wandered over the beautiful grounds together. Such lovely flowers, such fine trees, oh, how beautiful, how enchanting! Helen found herself indulging in her old dreams, and a rebellious wish arose that she might be rich, and enjoy such delightful things. But she already understood that what is God's will should be ours also. She did not yield to the discontent creeping over her, but lifting from her heart a prayer for contentment, gave herself up to the enjoyment of the hour.

How true are the Saviour's words, "It is more blessed to give than to receive." Mr. Nelson found pleasure in watching the joy of his youthful guests, as they ran and jumped and laughed, with perfectly childish glee. Although Helen and Barbara were fourteen, and Nora twelve, they were indeed children; for Mrs. Neville had never given them to understand that they would be young ladies at fifteen. In all such matters Mrs. Neville was very old-fashioned. She believed in keeping children children, and in lengthening out the sweet years of girlhood as long as possible.

"Ah," thought Mr. Nelson, with a sigh, "they are children yet, pure and true; they have not

15 *

mixed with the world, to learn its hypocrisy and deceit."

This was why he enjoyed their society, and tried to please them as he would never have tried to please older people. They went into the house, and there everything bespoke the refined taste of a gentleman, and the home of an intellectual epicure. They wandered from room to room, and listened to Mr. Nelson's stories of curiosities and pictures. But in the midst of it all, an exclamation from Helen turned all eyes in that direction.

"A harp! a harp!" she said joyfully, laying her hand caressingly upon it.

Her mind flew instantly to wild mountains, and an old grey-haired minstrel; it brought her home once more vividly before her.

"A harp!" said Nora. "Oh, Mr. Nelson, won't you please play us something?"

"I do not play, Nora, or I would willingly oblige you."

Now this harp had belonged to Mr. Nelson's mother, and had never been played upon since her death. Mr. Nelson had never heard it, and something of sacredness clung to it.

"I am very sorry," said Barbara; "I have read

so much about harps and I have never heard one."

"Never heard a harp?" said Helen, looking astonished; "ah, then you cannot know what you have missed."

Mr. Nelson smiled at Helen's enthusiasm, and said playfully, "Perhaps you can favor us with a tune, Helen?"

"Oh, will you indeed let me?" said Helen, eagerly. "I have not played since I left Scotland."

Mr. Nelson was surprised, and anything but pleased; but when Barbara and Nora both expressed their delight at Helen's being able to play, he reluctantly took off the cover. He had never heard a sound from his mother's harp, but in his boyish dreams he had connected all sweet sounds with it, and he did not like to have the spell broken by the careless twanging of a school girl. He almost made up his mind to leave the room, but sat down at the other end, while Nora and Barbara waited with breathless interest. It took Helen some time to tune it; but the instrument was a fine one, and the first chords that Helen struck convinced Mr. Nelson that she was a good player. But he was startled, as well as were Barbara and Nora, at the full, rich voice which burst forth into a Scottish song. The memory of old times was with her in that hour. She forgot the listeners, and sang with a passionate utterance of which she was unaware. She began with the free, wild song,

> "My heart's in the Highlands, my heart is not here,
> My heart's in the Highlands a chasing the deer;
> Chasing the wild deer, and following the roe,
> My heart's in the Highlands wherever I go."

Taught by the wandering Dugald, there was a boldness and force about her touch that accorded well with the wild music. Song followed song, for Mr. Nelson was a keen lover of music. And what music is like the human voice? Oh, ye who have the gift of song, use it for good; for nothing can so thrill and mould the heart as the rich sweetness of a fine voice.

Reluctantly Helen left the harp; but the afternoon was waning, and Mr. Nelson wished them to take another good play before supper, for as soon as that was over, they were to return home.

They went out to the woods. Mr. Nelson proposed "hide and seek," and joined in the game with a boyish ardor. Those grand old woods with their large trees, made splendid hiding-places. The game was a merry one, though rather warm.

"Oh, Barbara, isn't it splendid fun?" said Nora, as she came into "*baste*," her cheeks crimson with the exercise.

"Yes, it is very nice," said Mr. Nelson, smiling, "but days will end some time, and now I think it is time to rest before supper."

"Ah, but it's your turn to hunt," said Helen smiling, "and so I move we have just *one* more hide."

"Well then, just one more, as it is my turn; I'll soon find you."

"Now don't be too sure," said Helen, as she ran off.

Helen had noticed near the spot where they ate their dinner, a tree with very low branches, and she determined to get into that. She had on a dark chintz dress, and this would scarcely be seen among the thick leaves. She climbed pretty high up, and fixing herself comfortably, awaited, with many a little laugh, for Mr. Nelson to find her.

Barbara was soon found, then Nora; but to Helen's glee, she heard them all running, and hunting her, until fearing they might become

M

frightened, she whooped two or three times. This brought them all quite near her, but they never thought of looking up. At last, Helen, thinking they had searched long enough, dropped a leaf down, with a merry laugh. Mr. Nelson looked up; there was Helen's happy face looking down at him.

"See, you didn't find me so easily, after all," she said laughing, and starting to come down.

"Oh, Helen, how could you get up there?" asked Nora.

Mr. Nelson said nothing. It rather shocked his ideas of girlhood to find Helen climbing trees like a boy. He did not know how she had been brought up, almost wild, and that climbing a tree or a rock, was no more to Helen MacGregor, than lying down to rest.

He had been charmed by her singing and gay good humor, but this certainly lowered Helen very much in the eyes of the fastidious gentleman.

"Take care! Helen," he called out, "that limb is very unsafe."

But he spoke too late. The limb bent, then cracked, and Helen came rather heavily to the ground. She uttered a slight scream, quickly followed by a laugh. But Helen's merriment did not last long; Mr. Nelson lifted her up, and discovered that she had sprained her ankle.

He gently carried her to the house and laid her on a lounge. He then sent for the housekeeper, and being something of a doctor directed her what to do.

Mrs. Davis, the housekeeper, was a good woman, but very fussy. She made such a lament, and exclaimed so seriously over the accident while she was rubbing Helen's ankle, that Nora and Barbara were quite frightened.

"Oh, it will not be much," said Helen heroically, although the pain was very great.

"How will you get home?" said Nora, "your ankle is swelling so, you can't put on a shoe or stocking."

"I think I shall have to make her my prisoner for to-night and to-morrow," said Mr. Nelson kindly, "and then we will drive over to see you."

Helen tried to smile, and say she could go home; but it was as much as she could do to keep from crying whenever she moved her foot; so she concluded she had better stay.

A delicious little supper had been already prepared in the same place where they had taken
dinner; but as Helen could not go out, the table
was reset close to the lounge on which she was
lying. Mr. Nelson took supper with them, and
exerted himself to clear away the cloud that had
settled on the brows of his youthful guests.

Nora and Barbara were so sorry for Helen; and
Helen was dreading staying in that strange house
all night. But youth soon looks on the bright
side, and when it was time for Nora and Barbara
to go home, they were all in good spirits again.
Helen sent her love and a kiss to Mrs. Neville.
" And mind, Barbara, tell her not to be worried,
as I am better."

"Yes, we will," said Nora; "give me a kiss,
and I will be down in the morning to see how you
are, if mother is willing."

" Yes, do, Nora dear," she whispered, " for I
shall be dreadfully lonely. And, oh, Nora, water
my flowers, please, when you water yours."

" Yes, I will; good-bye."

" Just to think," said Nora, as she got into the
carriage, " that such a lovely day must be so short;
it seemed to be short, and yet when I think how

long it is since I saw mother, it seems to me quite long."

"Rather paradoxical that, Nora," said Mr. Nelson, laughing, "the day seems short, and yet it seems long."

Nora laughed too. "Yes, it is funny; but that is just the way it seems to me. We are so much obliged to you, Mr. Nelson; you took so much trouble to make us happy."

"And you, little Nora," he said, chucking her under the chin, "would be very apt to be happy, whether any one took trouble about you or not."

"Yes," said Nora, "but then mother says we ought to be happy, when God gives us so many, many blessings."

Mr. Nelson made no reply to this. Perhaps he thought, with some bitterness, that all his wealth could not give him a really happy moment; and he looked, with a sigh Nora could not understand, at her trusting face.

Mr. Nelson drove them home, and explained the accident to Mrs. Neville, telling her he would take good care of Helen.

And thus ended the happy day. Nora and Barbara could scarcely be got off to bed, they had so

much to tell; and Helen sank to sleep on a luxurious couch, in a handsome room, with a little sigh
of loneliness, missing the merry good nights of the
sisters, and she would willingly have exchanged
the costly magnificence of her chamber, for the
little bed in her own room.   It was a mark of the
growing change in Helen that she looked around
her with no wish to remain there.   She was learning under Mrs. Neville's teaching, to look upon
riches as they should be looked upon, only as a
great trust, giving us greater opportunities to further our Master's cause, and a mightier responsibility at the judgment day.

XIII.

HELEN AT OAKDALE.

"Think truly, and thy thoughts
  Shall the world's famine feed;
Speak truly, and each word of thine
  Shall be a faithful seed;
Live truly, and thy life shall be
  A great and noble creed."

HELEN'S visit to Oakdale, for that was the name of Mr. Nelson's place, proved anything but dull. She awoke the first morning with an earnest wish to go home, and a disagreeable idea of how long the day would be. But she little knew the many sources of pleasure that lay hidden in those vast rooms; and Mr. Nelson was far too kind to let his young guest suffer for want of amusement. There were portfolios full of the most exquisite engravings, the collection Mr. Nelson had made while travelling; books full of pictures and pleasant reading; rare curiosities and wonderful puzzles, over which Helen could have

spent days. Each morning Mrs. Davis assisted
her to the lounge by the open window which
looked out on the old-fashioned garden and deep
woods beyond. And then Mr. Nelson always
came in to pay what Helen called his "doctor's
visit;" but unlike other doctors, he always brought
something pleasant, a new book, or puzzle, or picture; and always left a dish of fine peaches beside
her on a little stand. No wonder then that the
three days' captivity passed very pleasantly to
Helen. Either Nora, or Barbara, or Mrs. Neville,
called every day; and finally Mrs. Neville on one
of her visits pronounced Helen well enough to
come home the next day, and Mr. Nelson had
promised to bring her in the carriage that afternoon. As she lay there on the lounge and gazed
idly out on the lovely landscape, she gave a little
sigh. To be sure she did wish to go home and
be with them all; but she could not help thinking
that there would be no Mrs. Davis there to pet
her and to wait on her, and no Mr. Nelson to
amuse her. The idea of work seemed rather dis-
tasteful. But Helen would not indulge herself in
such thoughts. She remembered in the Baptis
mal vow which she intended taking upon herself,

that she must promise to be contented in that state in which God had placed her, and she raised a sincere prayer for help to be enabled to go home cheerfully, and to return to her duties with none of the fault-finding spirit of other days. Helen had just regained her cheerful spirits once more, when Mr. Nelson entered.

"Well my little prisoner, this is your last morning here; this afternoon you get your release; and I expect you are very glad, too. It is rather dull, being shut up such lovely days."

"Oh, I have not been dull; how could I be when you have been so kind and have taken so much trouble for me? I am sure, sir, I shall never forget it. I do wish I could do something for you."

"Well, you can," said Mr. Nelson, smiling, "you can sing for me; and mind, I shall not be contented with one, two, or three songs. I must hear all I can now, as there is no telling when you will sprain your ankle again and have to stay here."

"Well," said Helen, laughing, "I do not mind the staying here, but I'd rather be excused from the sprain. Shall I go down stairs?"

16 *

"No, no, you must be a little careful yet; I will have the harp brought up."

The harp was brought and placed beside the lounge, and Helen was invited to sing. She was too little initiated into the fashions of society to wait to be coaxed until the pleasure of hearing is entirely destroyed by the trouble of obtaining. So Helen sang on, in her own fondness carried away by the spirit of the song, forgetful of her listener; only interrupted, if she paused, by Mr. Nelson's, "one more," until Helen looking up, smiling said, "Indeed I do not know another one."

"Not another one? Just think."

"Indeed I have thought, and I am sure I do not know any more."

"Well, then I suppose I must be contented; but who did teach you to play, Helen?"

"Dear old Dugald Stuart. He is one of those wandering harpers now almost gone from Scotland."

"He must be a fine player," said Mr. Nelson.

"Oh, if you could only hear him," said Helen, enthusiastically, "it seems to me I can see him now, with his long white hair, sitting on the rocks, harp in hand, and the dark pine trees, the blue loch, and the wild mountains around him. Ah, there is no land like Scotland. I love it."

Mr. Nelson smiled a little as he asked, "What makes you love it?"

"All things;" answered Helen promptly. "It is my native land, and the sky seems bluer, and the sunshine brighter. Through many childish years I wandered almost wild amidst its glens and mountains. I learned to love the grandeur of its wintry desolation, as well as the flowery beauty of its summer."

"Yes, I understand," said Mr. Nelson, "you love Scotland for its beauty, but that alone is a frail tenure to hold your love by."

"It has always been beautiful to me," replied Helen, "although many do not think with me there; but I love it better for the great and noble dead; for the free and independent spirit of its people. Tell me, when did the Scots ever submit tamely to subjugation? 'Tis the land of Wallace and of Bruce. Ah, if you were a Scotchman, you would not ask me why I love Scotland."

"I am Scotch," quietly said Mr. Nelson.

Helen almost jumped from the lounge, "Are you indeed Scotch? Oh, then you have been to

Scotland; you love it; and you know all about it, and I expect you have only been teasing me."

"Yes, I have been to Scotland, but I never lived there, for my parents brought me to this country when I was only six months old."

"Then you do not know what it is to live there," said Helen, a little disappointed.

"No," said Mr. Nelson, smiling, "but I think I prefer living in America. Do not misunderstand me though; I like Scotland, and the sturdy principles of its people. I also admire your two favorite heroes, Wallace and Bruce; although history says that Wallace was blood-thirsty, and Bruce the fickle and selfish earl of Carrick.

"Oh, do not say so," said Helen; "it was the proud nobility, who would not admit Wallace's superiority, that slandered him; and you must remember that when the earl of Carrick became king Robert the Bruce, he lost his follies, and was a noble king."

"Well, well, Helen, have your own way," said Mr. Nelson kindly, "I too have passed through the age of hero worship. While in Scotland I stood on the banks of the Carron, and in imagination heard the call of Wallace,

"Wake, earl of Carrick! wake to fame,
And make De Bruce the honored name!"

"You will understand, Helen, as you grow older, how all these things cease to interest."

"Do not tell me that; I can never believe that great and noble actions cease to charm and move our deepest feelings."

"They would not if they were found in the present; but great actions live only in the past. Do you think there are many women of the present day who would, like the beautiful Margaret Seaton, hold their arm in the staple of the door, until it was crushed, to defend their king?"

"Not *many*," said Helen, shrewdly, "and I dare say there were not many such in those days. But," she added timidly, "Mrs. Neville has taught me that there are actions performed just as heroically, and for nobler purposes, in these days, but they do not become historical."

"What, for instance?" asked Mr. Nelson, skeptically.

Helen blushed deeply; it was one thing to listen to, and imbibe Mrs. Neville's instructions and ideas, but quite another thing for one as inexperienced to tell them to the grave gentleman beside her, who she instinctively felt cared nothing for religion.

Mr. Nelson repeated the question, and Helen said,

"I cannot indeed make you understand, as Mrs. Neville could; but I was one day longing to live in heroic times, when she reminded me that all persons could redeem their lives from tameness, and make them heroic in self-sacrifice, by following the Saviour. She said too that there was many a heart struggle between duty and inclination far exceeding the physical sufferings which we read of and admire."

Helen stopped, for she saw Mr. Nelson did not relish the turn which the conversation was taking. Mr. Nelson admired the simple faith that could believe in such human goodness, but he had it not, and therefore it irritated him to hear of it; it seemed like a closed door which he could not enter, but always saw, and beyond which he felt certain lay the happiness he was ever craving. So without answering Helen's remark he went back to their former topic.

"How is it," he said, "you know so much about Scottish heroes? I thought you had never studied history."

"I am just beginning it," said Helen, smiling, "but I learned the history of Scotland's heroes in a much pleasanter way. Many a long winter evening I have sat and listened to old Margie's tales and legends of which I never tired. The peat fire would be our only light, and old Margie in a cap and short gown would knit industriously all the time, while I would sit listening and idly looking into the fire, imagining I could see there enacted all she was telling me. It was there I heard of the daring deeds of William Wallace; of the bravery of Robert Bruce; the fearful name of the black Douglass; the sorrows of the lovely Mary, Queen of Scotland; and many heroic legends of fair ladies, which live in the memories of the old and are handed down from generation to generation. It seemed to me last Sunday as though I was once more listening to old Margie when our rector spoke of the good Lord James of Douglass."

"Rather a strange subject for the pulpit," said Mr. Nelson, with a slight curl of the lip.

"Oh, no," said Helen, hastily, "not the way he used it; it was beautiful, and made me long to be what he said we should be."

"But how did he use it?" asked Mr. Nelson,

impelled to hear more of a subject that he was always shunning.

"Ah, I wish you could have heard him; I cannot tell it as he did, but I'll try and tell you what he meant. It was communion Sunday, and we don't have a sermon then, only a few remarks; and Mr. Clayton, after speaking of the wonderful love of Jesus, and of all he had done for us, said that King Robert Bruce on his death-bed requested the Earl of Douglass to take his heart to the Holy Land. Douglass had a silver case made in which he put the heart of Bruce, and wore it round his neck by a chain. On his way to the Holy Land, he stopped in Spain, and was persuaded to join in a battle against the Saracens. The Scots were defeated; and Douglass was so surrounded by Moors that he could not make his escape; so taking from his neck the heart of Bruce he flung it into the midst of the enemy, exclaiming, 'Forward, heart of Bruce! whither thou leadest, Douglass will follow or die,' and rushing forward to the place where it fell he was immediately killed. Then Mr. Clayton added, 'so the Christian should be willing devotedly to follow wherever Christ thinks best to lead him: whether into sorrow or trouble, or whatever adversity God thinks good for him, even though it be unto death. For after all, that was only a fulfilment of the prayer we pray every day, 'Thy will be done.' Can you understand my poor way of telling it, Mr. Nelson?"

"Very well. You have a good memory, Helen."

"Yes, I have."

Mr. Nelson was rather amused at this frank admission. But if he had said, "Helen, you are pretty," she most likely would have acknowledged that as well; for Helen knew too little of the ways of the world to know that it is fashionable to tell an untruth rather than to say anything favorable of yourself. In the same way she talked freely with any one; not that she was bold, or forward, but she liked to talk, and had never been taught "that little girls must be seen and not heard." And at Mrs. Neville's cottage, religion was so thoroughly the every day life of the family, that to talk of it seemed only natural.

"It is strange," said Mr. Nelson after a pause, "that such a zealous admirer of Scotland can be content here. Don't you long to go back?"

"I did," answered Helen; "I do not now."

17   N

"And why not now?"

"Because," she replied, "although it was pleasant to lead the life I led, yet there I never went to Sunday-school; I never heard of a better and happier life. There are plenty of Sunday-schools there; but my father would not allow me to go."

"The same subject," thought Mr. Nelson; and taking out his watch he said, "I must go now; be ready to start at five o'clock; and mind, I shall expect to hear that good-bye song before we go."

"Yes," said Helen laughing, "I shall sing it so sadly that you'll begin to cry."

"If I do you will certainly be frightened," said Mr. Nelson as he went out.

Helen remained alone; she ate her dinner, looked over the pictures, and tried all the puzzles once more; practised a little on the harp, and five o'clock came all too soon. Helen sang the good-bye song, and although Mr. Nelson laughed, instead of crying, yet he felt far more sorry to part with Helen than she supposed. He led a lonely life; Helen had a good memory, and a Highlander's gift of talking well, and she entertained him. Then too "the innocence and truth of early youth still lingered around her;" and Mr. Nelson

had seen too much of the world not to prize those
fleeting hours.   Helen had also the greatest of all
charms, true religion; and in spite of his skepticism, as Mr. Nelson drove home, after leaving
Helen at the cottage, he sighed for the pure faith
and Christian life which he saw practised there.
Helen's words, too, still haunted him.   He had
been a great dreamer; he had longed to do some
great thing, that should make him rank among
the "few immortal names that were not born to
die."   But the true heroism of duty fulfilled at
any cost, the beauty of self-sacrifice, the high mis-
sion of a Christ follower, the wish to have his
name written on the roll of honor in the court of
heaven, and ever show a firm loyalty to Jehovah
Jesus, the King of kings,—of all these he had never
truly thought until Mr. Clayton's illustration had
waked them into life.   And as Mr. Nelson entered
Oakdale, he said with Agrippa of old, "Almost
thou persuadest me to be a Christian."

XIV.

THE TEA-PARTY.

"Not long does the life blood career through the heart:
  Like the glory of summer we come and depart;
  Yet, e'en like that glory, if gentle and kind,
  We leave both a beauty and fragrance behind."

HOW hard it is to settle down to the routine of every day duties after indulgence in a pleasant visit, or a holiday! Helen found it particularly so after her return home. She awoke the next morning with a disappointed feeling, and a sense of something pleasant gone, which made the things around her lose their usual charm. But Helen knew that discontent was a sin; and kneeling down, she prayed earnestly for a cheerful, contented spirit. And the Saviour heard and answered. She arose, determined to think no more of Oakdale, and its easy life. But when she went down stairs, and was met by Nora with a hearty kiss, and the lively exclamation, "Oh, Helen, I have something so splendid to tell you," the last cloud vanished, and she entered into the plans proposed with a delight that dispelled all thoughts of regret.

Nora's important news was, that Monday was Barbara's birth-day, and they would have a tea-party as they always had on their birth-days.

"And doesn't it happen well?" said Nora; "Barbara's birth-day comes in August, and mine in January; so we always have two parties a year. When does yours come, Helen?"

"Why, in January too,—the first."

"Oh dear, and mine is the eighth, that would be too close together."

"You and Helen will have to celebrate yours the same day," said Mrs. Neville.

"Yes," said Nora, "I suppose we will; but you see, mother, I was in hopes we'd get *three.*"

"I am so sorry you can't walk much yet, Helen," said Barbara, "for we are going out to invite the girls this afternoon, and we wanted you to go with us."

Helen looked disappointed; girls enjoy inviting company so much.

"Don't you think you could go with us if we sat down to rest often?" asked Nora.

17 *

"Where would we sit down?" said Barbara, laughing.

"Oh, on the road-side, or door-steps; you know that would be allowable when we are taking an invalid out."

There is no knowing what the invalid would have said, but Mrs. Neville interfered,

"If Helen wishes to run and play on Monday, she had better keep quiet until then, so that her ankle will feel strong again."

This decided the question; the fear of not being able to play on Monday gave Helen courage to watch Nora and Barbara depart, without a sigh.

While they were gone Mr. Nelson called to see how his patient was; and on hearing of the girls' proposed tea-party he asked Mrs. Neville's permission to send them some of his fine peaches. He took delight in gratifying his young friends, for he loved to see their eyes sparkle, and their cheeks flush with joy, and to hear their warm thanks. So on Monday, when the peaches came, Mrs. Neville was not surprised to see in addition a large pitcher of cream, and three handsome bouquets of flowers. On one was written "Barbara," on another "Helen," and on the third "Nora." They were just alike, excepting that the top flower of Helen's was a magnificent white lily. It was the only one in bloom, and Mr. Nelson had hesitated some time whose name to write on it, but at length decided on Helen's. So it was determined that this bouquet should stand in the centre of the supper table, and Nora's and Barbara's at each end. Flowers out of their own garden, already decorated the parlor.

The girls enjoyed themselves vastly arranging the tea-table before they went up to dress, thus saving their mother as much work as possible.

Fifteen plates Barbara put down; Nora followed with fifteen knives, and Helen with fifteen forks; and so they counted everything.

"You fix the napkins in the goblets, Helen," said Nora, "because you do it so nicely."

Helen complied; and then they all stood off to admire the table, until admonished by Mrs. Neville that it was time to dress.

Helen's ankle was quite well, and she ran down stairs as eagerly as any to welcome the youthful guests. There were all Mrs. Neville's Sunday-school class, eight girls, two others from the village, and Mary Rellim. Mrs. Neville had hesi-

tated a little about inviting Mary, but since Gussie's death Mrs. Rellim had sent Mary to the
cottage several times, either to ask some favor, or
to pay a visit, and Mrs. Neville did not wish to
repulse these friendly overtures. Mary came,
dressed a great deal too extravagantly for the occasion, which was meant to be a real play time.
Mrs. Neville always threw open the whole house,
excepting the dining room and kitchen. They
might hide from the garret to the cellar, and exercise their youthful lungs to the utmost.

Helen, Barbara, and Nora, wore simple light
chintz dresses fit to play in. And as several of the
girls were quite poor, Mrs. Neville did not wish
her girls to dress in a manner that would make
them feel uncomfortable. Many of the girls had
looked with rather envious eyes on Mary Rellim's
pink barege and its tiny flounces trimmed with
silk; but, long before the afternoon was over, it
would have been difficult to get any of that little
company to exchange dresses with her. For Mary
would play; and running through the bushes in
the excitement of "tagger," or hiding in closets,
and behind doors, was rather hard on barege; so
that poor Mary was constantly running to some

one to get her dress pinned up. And by the time they had gone through all the noisy plays Mary was by no means the best dressed girl in the room, as she had determined she would be.

"I am real sorry you have torn your dress so," said Helen, as she stood by Mary during one of the plays.

"Oh, it makes no difference," carelessly answered Mary.

"It is a pity you did not think to wear a dress that would not tear so easily," said Helen, without intending to say anything unpleasant; but Mary was out of humor with her misfortunes, and she answered sneeringly,

"I ought to have worn *calico*, I suppose. You think because you can't afford to wear anything else, nobody should."

In an instant anger flashed from Helen's eyes, and she answered haughtily,

"A barege dress never yet made a *lady* of the person who wore it."

She did not wait for Mary's reply, but turned angrily away. But if Helen's temper had been quick, so also was her repentance. The thought shot through her with a thrill of pain, "I have been angry. I have sinned. O my Saviour, forgive me!" And without stopping an instant she ran out to the porch, where Mary had just gone, and said, " Do forgive me, Mary ; I get angry so quickly, and I forget myself; it was very unkind in me. Won't you try and forget it, and enjoy yourself?"

Mary Rellim was very much surprised at this termination of a quarrel which she expected would be like the many they used to have; but although surprised, she was unable to appreciate the frank avowal and its generous wish. She felt angry, and took no trouble to conceal it ; and it took all Helen's efforts for the rest of the afternoon, which she zealously devoted to Mary, to restore the sullen beauty to a good humor ; and it was accomplished then only by a mere accident which Helen took advantage of. They had exhausted all their lively plays and some one proposed " cross questions." This was hailed with pleasure. They seated themselves in two rows, facing each other; then one went through the centre asking questions ; if she asked a question of one girl, the one opposite to her had to answer it immediately, or pay a forfeit; and the selling of these forfeits formed a very merry part of the game. Lucy Dean was selling the forfeits over Barbara's head.

"Heavy, heavy, what hangs over?" asked Lucy.

"Fine, or superfine?"

"Superfine; what must be done with the owner?"

"She must bow to the prettiest, kneel to the wittiest, and kiss the one she loves best," said Barbara.

"Here, here, Helen, it is yours," said several eager voices.

Helen advanced, took her pocket handkerchief, and then looked round on the little circle with criticizing eyes. She made eye-glasses of her fingers, declaring that she must be very particular; then crossing the room she bowed very low to Mary Rellim; she knelt before Edith Ray, the oldest, and therefore supposed to be the wittiest; and then, throwing her arms around Nora, gave her a hearty kiss. That was the added rose-leaf to Nora's brimming cup of happiness that afternoon. She loved Helen so much, that although it was only a play, she felt anxious to know whom she would kiss.

The bow vanquished the ill nature of Mary Rellim, and Helen could enjoy herself for the rest of
the time. Her hasty temper, and her regret at
giving way to it, had cast a gloom over her spirits,
though she strove to hide it for the sake of her
guests. But now she felt relieved once more, that
she had atoned, as far as she was able, for her
fault, and Mary Rellim had condescended so far
as to speak to her.

Many other forfeits were sold, for each girl had
several. One had to propose a new play, another
to perform a piece on the piano, a third to tell a
comic story, and so on, each one adding her mite
to the general entertainment. At length it came
Helen's turn again to pay a forfeit.

"Indeed," said Barbara, who was the seller this
time, "I can't think of another thing; tell me
what I shall ask the unfortunate owner to do."

"Tell her to go out of the room for five minutes,
and then come in and do something to amuse the
company," suggested Edith Ray.

"Well then, I hope it's yours, Edith," said
Mary Rellim.

But no, it was Helen's. She took it very reluctantly and went out of the room, having no

idea what to do. But Mrs. Neville always taught
her children to use every exertion in their power
to entertain their guests. If any girl did not wish
to do a thing, one of them always offered at once
to take her place. True hospitality reigned at the
cottage. The desire of a guest, expressed, when
right, was law; so Helen made up her mind that
she could not back out, but must think of something. Five minutes elapsed, and she did not
come. Ten minutes, and still no Helen. The
waiting ones begin to grow impatient, when lo! the
door flies open, and in bounds Helen, dressed as a
Highland maid! Not the way she usually dressed
when at home, but in a suit which had been her
grandmother's when she was a girl, and which
Helen insisted, in spite of Margaret's entreaties, on
bringing with her. She wore a dark blue jacket
and short skirt. A scarlet plaid was fastened on
one shoulder, and knotted on the other side at her
waist, the ends hanging down to the bottom of her
skirt. Her feet and ankles were bare, and her
simple head-dress consisted of a scarlet snood, over
which her dark hair hung in heavy ringlets.
Helen made a graceful little bow, and then broke
forth into a gay Scottish song. When she had

18

finished, without waiting an instant, she bowed again and sprang out of the door near which she stood. All the girls called, and then started after her; but they called and pleaded in vain, Helen could not be found. After a fruitless search they returned to the parlor, and there she sat quietly reading!

Great was the laughing, and many the exclamations, which were only increased by Helen's perfectly grave face, and serious questions as to what was the matter.

"Ah, Helen, I think you might have stayed longer." "Did you use to dress so?" "How splendid you did look!" "Where *did* you go?" Thus the questions eagerly went on; but no entreaties would induce Helen to appear again. She had dressed and undressed in the kitchen, with Mrs. Neville's help; and the doors were locked that led to that and the dining-room, and Mrs. Neville had advised her not to spoil the first effect by a second appearance; so at length they settled down. Only one more forfeit remained to be sold.

"I do wish that was yours, Helen," said Lucy Dean, "and then perhaps you would sing again."

But it proved to be Nora's.

"She must tell a serious story," said Barbara.

"What kind of a serious story?" asked Nora.

"Oh, a ghost story," said Lucy Dean.

"A ghost story!" exclaimed several girls at once, "there are no such things as ghosts."

"I have heard of ghosts," said Helen.

"So have I," said Nora, "and I will tell you a real ghost story."

"Now, Nora," said Barbara, "how can you? You know there are no ghosts."

"Very well, Barbara, just wait and hear; Aunt Stella told it to me; she read it in the paper and of course it must be true."

"It can't be bad if Aunt Stella told it," said Barbara.

"Once upon a time," began Nora,—Here all the girls laughed.

"Well, you know I must begin somehow, and I don't know any other beginning. So, once upon a time, there was a clergyman lived in the West of England, who used to take a few boys to educate. At this time he had five pupils at his house. The clergyman's family consisted of himself, wife, son, and daughter, but the son was away at college. The house was not very large, but part of

it was not used, because it was so old and dilapi-
dated. Now on one side of the house, on the first
floor, was the school-room and play-room; over
the school-room was the boys' bed-room, and next
to that an empty room which was in bad condi-
tion and never used; and over that again an
empty garret, with broken windows and falling
plaster. The other side of the house was occupied
by the clergyman and his family. The boys' bed-
room had a door which opened into the empty
room, and a few steps and a trap door, led into the
garret.

"One day the whole family went out for a long
walk, and took their dinners with them. When
the boys went to bed that night, they found the
door leading into the empty room open; but they
did not think much of that; they shut it, and then
went to sleep. Suddenly, they were all wakened
by a loud scream in the empty room. They could
not think what it was; then some one said it was
only fancy; when the youngest said, fearfully,
'Could it be a ghost?'

"'Nonsense,' said Dean, the oldest boy, 'you
surely do not believe in ghosts, Edwards.'

"So they all commenced to tease poor little Edwards, and he insisted it was a ghost, and dared any of them to go in; but they were all afraid. At length, the two eldest, ashamed, got up, put on a few clothes, and opened the door of the empty room; they looked in; nothing was to be seen; the moonlight poured in at the empty window and made everything look cold and dismal. Then one of the boys, safe in bed, called out, 'look in the garret.' Dean went up the steps, and while he was lifting up the trap door the three boys in the bed-room ventured as far as the door to see what would happen. No sooner had Dean opened the trap door than they all saw something white glide past, and heard the same piercing scream. Dean uttered a scream also, and in his fright let the trap door fall on his head; this stunned him so that he fell down on the other boy Walker, and knocked him down, and they both rolled over together. Dean was insensible, and Walker was too much afraid of the ghost to move. In the mean time, the other three boys jumped into bed and covered their heads all up, expecting every moment some horrid ghost would rush in and carry them off. Mr. Staunton was awakened by the noise, and came in to see what was the matter. 'Oh, sir, the ghost! the ghost!' was all the boys could say. He went into the other room and brought out Dean and Walker, and stayed with the boys the rest of that night and the next night, but nothing more was heard."

" Well, what was it?" asked Lucy.

" Why a ghost, of course," answered Julia Mayberry, who had a very superstitious mother.

" Well," continued Nora, "everything remained quiet; and at last the boys gained courage to sleep by themselves, and Mr. Staunton left them. But about a month after the first alarm, they heard noises as if some one was scratching in the garret; several nights after they heard shrieks, quite distinctly. They called for Mr. Staunton each time, and he went up into the garret, but although he thought he heard a rustling, he could see nothing. On the next day, Edward Staunton, the son, came home from college, and was very much surprised to hear of the ghost. He told the boys to call him as soon as they heard any noise. They did; he went quietly up the ladder, and opened the trap door; they heard a great fluttering, sounds of shrieks redoubled, a sound of breaking glass, and a violent struggle, and then Edward called out that he had found the ghost; he came down the ladder, bringing with him, what do you think?"

"What? what?" asked all the girls eagerly.

"A fine large owl!"

The burst of laughter that followed this was only interrupted by the tea-bell; and both Helen and Julia were glad to escape the teasing they got about the ghost.

Never did a tea-table look more inviting, with its flowers and fruit, and seldom was one better appreciated. After supper the evening was spent in singing and music. They sang hymns towards the last, and Mrs. Neville read a chapter in the Bible and prayed. Thus separated this happy party. No ill humor marred their good-byes, and they were sorry the afternoon was so soon over.

XV.

"My child, the counsels high attend
Of thy Eternal Friend.
When longings pure, when holy prayers,
When self-denying thoughts and cares
　　Room in thy heart would win,
Stay not too long to count them o'er;
Rise in his name; throw wide the door;
　　Let the good angels in."

THE world is full of beauty; and life is very sweet, even to the care-worn. Helen's lot had been cast in the midst of pleasant scenes. Her young feet had been free to wander amongst the trees and flowers, to climb the mountain path and search the shaded dell, and to rove, like a child of nature as she was, where Nature was most beautiful to her every sense. And now, removed from the scenes of her wild, untutored childhood, in the orderings of a kind Providence she was receiving almost a mother's love and care from Mrs. Neville; and enjoying a true and refining friendship

212

in Nora and Barbara. But more than all this, Helen had found the Saviour. Each day she was living closer and closer to him. Religion was more to her than a mere name; it was becoming the daily guide of her life, an unfailing source of blessing whether in joy or trouble. "The lines" had indeed "fallen to her in pleasant places," and she had "a goodly heritage." But each life-cup holds its share of sorrow. Helen could not forget that she did not hear from her father.

The summer had passed away, and October, with its brilliant beauty and evanescent glory, crowned the earth. Helen had at first watched eagerly for a letter, but hope had at length died out. Her spirit was too independent to allow her to remain long a burden to others, after she began to realize the true position of things. She therefore made up her mind to become a teacher; and with redoubled energy entered upon her studies in the beginning of September. Naturally of a sunny temper, and not given to much sadness of spirit, Helen yet bore a real grief about with her, on account of her father. Although she had never loved him with the deepest affection, and although their parting had been without a pang on her part, she could not help feeling sometimes, with a saddened heart, that she might never see him again. Then too, she had her hours of soul despondency, (as what Christian has not?) when she thought of what she should be, of what her Saviour expected her to be, and of what she was not.

At such times how the trustful soul throws itself on the compassion of an infinite love, and finds consolation in the thought of the gentleness of that Saviour who will not "break the bruised reed, nor quench the smoking flax!"

One morning Helen felt particularly sad. It was the day before they had attended the funeral of Lucy Dean's father; and she had watched, with a keen pang, the passionate sorrow of the bereaved orphans over him who had been so tender and so kind. She heard friends speaking of his devotion to his motherless children, and a yearning wish filled her heart that she also might taste a father's love, while the bitter thought would come with it that *her* father did not care enough for her even to send after her, but had willingly abandoned her to the care of strangers. When Helen arose the morning after the funeral, something of this sadness still lingered, but it was mingled with a thought more absorbing. What was to become of Lucy Dean and her five little brothers and sisters? They had talked over it the evening before, and Mrs. Neville had said it would be impossible for her to do much; and Helen noticed that she said it with deep regret. Instantly the thought occurred,—"She could do more for those friendless ones if it were not for me. *I* am the additional burden that hinders her. Then, too, Lucy is in her Sunday-school class, and therefore has a greater claim on her help." This thought worried Helen, and she could not recover her spirits. Nora and Barbara playfully rallied her on her melancholy face.

They were taking in their flowers for the winter,—always a delightful task for Nora and Barbara. Helen participated in it for the first time, and Nora had predicted that she would greatly enjoy it. And Helen did enjoy it, but the trace of sadness still lingered with it all.

"Three of these windows have the sun all winter," said Barbara; "which will you have, Helen?"

"Either one," answered Helen, placing a magnificent rose-bush on the wide window ledge; "flowers are very lovely, but so frail; they cannot bear the least cold breath."

"Well," said Nora, "for my part I am glad they cannot. Just to think, if flowers lived out all winter, we could not have them in the house to make it beautiful when all is desolate out of doors; and we would not have the pleasure of taking them up."

"Nor the pleasure of getting quite muddy from head to foot," said Mrs. Neville, smiling.

Nora laughed heartily as she glanced from her mud-stained dress to her mud-covered fingers; but Mrs. Neville noticed that Helen did not, as usual, join in the laugh, but that she stood bending over a heliotrope with a sort of absent air. Nora and Barbara had already returned to the garden, and Mrs. Neville going up to Helen, said gently,

"You seem to be sad to-day, dear Helen; what is the matter?"

Helen, who had been striving to conquer her feelings all the morning, had now arrived at that point when a few kind words completely overcame her, and bursting into tears she said,

"Oh, Mrs. Neville, I know you could do something for Lucy Dean if it were not for me. How I wish I did not have to be a burden to you."

"Helen! Helen!" said her kind benefactor, half reproachfully, and yet tenderly, "how *can* you talk so?" and drawing the young girl to her she kissed her fondly. "Are you not my daughter, adopted as my own, and loved far better than Lucy could be? Do you not repay me ten-fold daily for the little I do for you?"

"Oh, yes," said Helen, warmly returning the caresses, "but I know you long to help Lucy, and"—

"And I intend to help her."

"But you are not able to do all that you wish, for her."

"Can we *ever* do all we wish? Our duty, Helen dear, is to do all that we *can;* and surely both you and I have faith enough to leave the rest to God,—to that God who has proclaimed himself the Father of the fatherless."

"Ah, if I had but your faith, dear Mrs. Neville! I so often doubt. Sometimes I feel as though I could trust God for everything; and then again all looks dark and I think I must rely on human help."

19

"Alas, Helen, that is human weakness, the world over. Now 'we see through a glass, darkly,' but there comes a time when 'we shall see face to face,' when the faith of earth, poor, weak, and frail as it is, shall be lost in the all-glorious reality of heaven. Until then, we must pay the penalty of humanity, and strengthen our feeble faith by unceasing draughts from the fount of life. 'We must draw up living water, with the golden chain of prayer.' Ay, and this very weakness throws us more entirely upon our Saviour. You will find, dear Helen, that life is a continued warfare between good and evil, between duty and inclination. I know it is hard sometimes to bear our little troubles and vexations, but happy are they who through Christ's strength come out triumphant, and 'having respect unto the recompense of the reward,' 'count all things but loss for the excellency of the knowledge of Christ.' You remember the words of our favorite poet?—

> "'Oh, thou so weary of thy self-denials,
>   And so impatient of thy little cross,
>   Is it so hard to bear thy daily trials,
>   To count thy earthly things a gainful loss?
>   What if thou *always* suffer tribulation,
>   And if thy Christian warfare *never* cease?

The gaining of the quiet habitation,
　　Shall gather thee to everlasting peace.'"

Helen felt greatly encouraged by Mrs. Neville's words. There was comfort in knowing that others also, at times, felt their faith grow weak; yet she could not give up the idea of assisting Mrs. Neville in some way to aid the orphan family. When therefore the flowers were all brought in, and Mrs. Neville expressed her intention of going to see Lucy, and asked Helen if she would like to go with her, she gladly accepted the invitation. Before starting, however, she knelt down and prayed, that if consistent with his will, God would show her some way of helping these poor children, and also of manifesting her gratitude to Mrs. Neville for all her tender care. Helen's communion with her Saviour was not in vain. She rose from her knees feeling assured that at the right time he would open to her the door of opportunity and give her grace to enter it. Nora and Barbara would have liked very much to go too, but their mother had simply asked Helen, and they had been trained from childhood to acquiesce in her decisions without inquiring the why and the wherefore. Nora ran after Helen to the gate to

thrust a balsam apple into her hand, charging her
to be sure and tell Lucy to put some liquor on it
and keep it, as it was so excellent if any of the
children should fall down and hurt themselves.
Helen took it and promised, but she could not
help wondering in her mind where Lucy would
get the liquor.

They found Lucy, with all the family gathered
round her, busily darning stockings. She was
very glad that they had come, but received them
with such a hopeless, dejected manner, that it went
to Mrs. Neville's heart. The sun shone cheerfully
into the room, and the youngest children were
having a romp on the floor; but nothing seemed
to dispel the despondent cloud from the brow of
the slender girl, who busily working with a woman's patience, had even in these sad moments, to
lay aside her sorrow, and to attend to the pressing
necessities of poverty. She brightened up a little,
however, when Mrs. Neville asked after each of
the children, and when Helen insisted that there
never was a sweeter little fellow than the baby,
which she took on her lap at once. Lucy also
thought that there were few better children, and
she began telling Mrs. Neville of some of their

endearing qualities. There were Laura and Susie who were a great help to her. Laura could sweep and dust and make the beds, and Susie always washed the dishes, while Aleck and Tom brought the water and kindling wood. "As for baby, darling," continued Lucy, "he can only be funny yet, and not very useful, but we all love him so."

"Baby darling," who was two years old, immediately showed his appreciation of these remarks by sticking out his little bare toes towards the fire and shouting loudly, "papa, papa." Tears dimmed Lucy's eyes at the dear name, and little Tom, stealing softly behind her, put his arms round her and said soothingly,

"Don't cry, Lucy, I'll soon be a man, and then I'll be papa for you."

Lucy drew him fondly to her side and brushed back the hair from his pretty forehead.

"Oh," said she, "if I only could keep them together a while, until they get a little older."

"Have you thought of any way that it might be done?" asked Mrs. Neville kindly.

"No, ma'am; dear father left only a few dollars. You know winter before last, when mother died, he was sick nearly all the time, and the money

19 *

he had laid up all went. Since then he could not save much, for I am not the good housekeeper that mother was."

"Still," said Mrs. Neville, "I think something can be done; we must hope and pray for the best. I feel that you know to whom to go for strength and help."

"Yes, ma'am," said Lucy, "were it not for the dear Saviour's help and guidance, I know I could not succeed in anything. Dear papa said just before he died, 'Lucy, my daughter, Jesus will never forsake you. Pray to him.' And this morning it seemed to me as I was thinking of those words, a sudden hope filled my heart."

Helen's tears had flowed in sympathy with Lucy's, and she said earnestly, "Don't you think, Lucy, you could do enough plain sewing to buy bread for these little ones? You would not need much more, for you have potatoes and apples put away for all winter."

"I was thinking of that; and I might make out, for the children could do the house work, if it were not for the rent. I could not earn enough to pay that too, and I have only twenty-five dollars."

"And winter is coming, and little feet require shoes," said Mrs. Neville; "but don't be discouraged, Lucy; we will see what can be done. All these little ones are the children of 'the righteous,' whom, the Psalmist declares, he has 'not seen forsaken, nor his seed begging bread.'"

"Who is the landlord, Lucy?" Helen asked abruptly.

"Mr. Nelson, and he is very strict."

"Mr. Nelson!" said Helen, almost clapping her hands for joy. "Oh, then you can stay, Lucy; he will not ask you any rent."

"Helen," said Mrs. Neville, "do not cheer Lucy with that thought. Mr. Nelson is, as Lucy says, a strict landlord, and will require all the rent."

Lucy sighed, but Helen only smiled. It seemed impossible to her generous nature, that a man as rich as Mr. Nelson should be anxious for the rent of one poor cottage. Older persons, more worldly wise than Helen, could have told her that the poor, as a general rule, give more liberally in proportion to their ability, than the rich. But it is hard to chill the ardent faith of youth. Mrs. Neville's arguments on the way home did not dampen Helen's zeal. She was too proud by nature to ask a favor for herself; but for the orphan little ones she had just left, she determined to conquer her feelings, and go early Monday morning to Mr. Nelson herself.

Nora and Barbara shared Helen's enthusiasm; and they had planned out together quite a life of ease, for Lucy. They agreed to mend and make all the children's clothes at their weekly Dorcas, when they were unpleasantly reminded by Mrs. Neville that Lucy could not earn enough to buy the children new clothes, that there were not many in Brookfield who gave out plain sewing, and Mrs. Neville knew that it would take much exertion on her part to induce those few to patronize a girl as young as Lucy. She explained all this to the girls, and thus suddenly demolished their beautiful air-castles. This did not, however, completely discourage them. They soon rallied again, and set themselves busily to thinking.

"Never mind," said Nora, with a little sigh of disappointment, "we will manage it somehow."

"I am sure we will," said Helen.

Busy as thought was, however, no conclusion could be arrived at to raise money sufficient to buy shoes and comfortable clothes for the children the next winter.

"If it were only summer time," said Barbara, "we might raise vegetables in our gardens and sell them."

But as it was not summer time, that would not do. At length, after the supper dishes were washed, and Nora had said that she was almost ready to give up, and Barbara had declared that her head ached thinking, Helen said slowly,

"I know how we can do it."

"How? how?" eagerly inquired both girls.

But the plan Helen had thought of required an amount of self-sacrifice that prevented her telling it with all the joy that the others expected. For the last two hours she had tried to banish the thought as impracticable, and had only just now, after a silent prayer for strength, made up her mind to propose her plan. Mrs. Neville had promised to buy them each a silk dress the coming winter. Helen knew that these dresses were to cost twelve dollars a piece; and she knew that the merino ones which they were to have had would cost but six. Now the thought would intrude itself that if each of the girls could only make up her mind to be satisfied with the merinoes, there would be a sum of eighteen dollars saved, which would be enough to clothe the children comfortably. But then, Helen had never in her life had a silk dress, and she had looked on Mary Rellim's many a time with longing eyes. No one can appreciate what the sacrifice was to Helen, unless like her, she is extravagantly fond of handsome clothes. We all know how Helen, from the injudicious training of her childhood, had learned to look on wealth and rank as everything. Through the sweet teachings of gospel truth she had ceased to care for the wealth of this world, and had placed her treasure in heaven; but many of Helen's faults still clung to her; she sometimes found herself lingering before the looking-glass and recalling Dugald's praises; and the idea of a silk dress had filled her with delight. But Helen was now to learn that "It is more blessed to give than to receive." Every regret vanished as she met Mrs. Neville's approving smile, and heard Nora's joyous exclamation,

"Why, Helen, you are the queen of thinkers. I never thought of the silk dresses; how stupid of me!"

And that was true of Nora. Dress was always a secondary consideration with her; and she had many a time gone to church in a calico without caring in the least. Barbara's answer did not come quite as readily as Nora's. Like Helen, the first silk dress in anticipation had many attractions for her. But she would not hold back alone, and so it was decided upon. Mrs. Neville, however, suggested that Lucy would feel much more comfortable if she worked for the money, than if she received it as a gift; and as she had some sheets to make up she proposed giving them to her to do at her leisure, paying her liberally in shoes and clothes. This delighted the girls, and in their minds Lucy was already fixed comfortably for the winter. Not a doubt troubled them as to Mr. Nelson's answer.

Oh the generous faith of youth! Would that we all could carry more of its beauty and freshness to the noontide of life, and to the evening of age! A perennial fount of blessing springing up in the desert wastes of the world, never dried by the heat of passion nor drained by the draughts of selfishness and avarice!

XVI.

THE REQUEST.

"He is not worthy to hold from heaven
The trust reposed, the talents given,
Who will not add to the portion that's scant,
In the pinching hours of cold and want."

THERE are some dispositions naturally patient; they can wait, and wait calmly, days, months, and even years, for the attainment of a darling wish. Others, naturally impatient, have, through the all-powerful influence of religion, learned to curb desire, and to imitate their divine Master. Helen MacGregor was like the mountain stream of her native land, swift and impetuous and impatient of restraint. Years had not yet given to her character that Christian completeness which the Saviour's true disciples must eventually attain. Glad and joyous youth was hers, and youth is ever impatient to overleap all obstacles and reach the goal at once. Thus Helen entered the study on Monday morning for the first time in weeks, with

a cloud on her brow. Mrs. Neville had refused
to let her go to Mr. Nelson's until after the study
hour in the afternoon. This was not much of a
trial, to be sure, but to Helen's disposition it was
a great disappointment. She had fully made up
her mind to start the first thing in the morning;
and Helen had been her own mistress too long not
to feel keenly the least restraint. She entered the
study looking angry, and feeling rebellious. But
Helen knew well that it is the small, insignificant
acts and feelings, of every day, that go to swell the
long list of Christian virtues, or Christian failings.
Every evil thought conquered wins a smile from
heaven. And day by day to come out victors
through Christ, over the petty vexations of life,
shall at last place our feet on the golden pavement, and wreathe our brows with the crown immortal. Helen sat down at her desk with a bitter
feeling, but it did not last long. She saw lying on
her book two of Nora's choicest flowers. Sympathy is like the genial sunshine; it wakens into
beauty all our better feelings. Tears fell on
Helen's open geography, as she thought, "How
wicked, oh, how wicked I am, to get angry over
such a trifle. Dear Saviour, make me more

20

worthy of being thy child;" and leaning her head on the desk she prayed to be forgiven, and for strength to overcome. The cloud was gone; dispelled, as all the Christian's clouds must ever be, by communion with her Saviour.

" Dear Nora," thought Helen, "how sweet she is; she wanted to cheer me, and so she picked her choicest flowers for me." Helen looked up, and catching Nora's eye she kissed the flowers, and smiled her thanks. Nora returned the smile, happy to think that Helen was once more herself. And well was it for Helen that she overcame that first disappointment in the right way, and sought for grace and strength; for that day was to contain many disappointments. Lessons and dinner were at length over, and the quiet of the study hour reigned in the little school-room. Helen glanced impatiently at the clock. Only half an hour more. Mrs. Neville had excused her from sewing. Only half an hour. Helen's mind wandered from the lesson; she looked out at the crimson leaves flying before the wind, when suddenly Mr. Nelson opened the gate. Helen could scarcely believe it. Yes, it was he. She forgot the "quiet rule," and exclaimed,

"Oh, there is Mr. Nelson now!"

Barbara looked out of the window, and then resumed her grammar. Nora did not raise her head from her slate. Helen continued,

"I wonder if I could go out and ask him now?"

This was too much for Nora; in anxiety to save Helen from disobeying, she exclaimed hastily,

"Oh, don't, Helen; mother will call you if she thinks best."

"I wonder,"—began Helen, but Nora put her finger on her lip, and bent once more over her slate.

Helen smiled and nodded and sat down to her lesson; but she could not study; she was expecting every minute to be called, and thinking what she should say. But she had her trouble for nothing; Mrs. Neville did not call her, and Helen, with a sigh of disappointment, saw Mr. Nelson go away. She watched him till he was out of sight, and forgot to look at her book until she was suddenly roused by Mrs. Neville's entrance, and Barbara's exclamation as she ran out of the room, "Study hour is over."

"Oh, why didn't you call me?" asked Helen.

"Trust me, Helen," said Mrs. Neville; "I know Mr. Nelson best, and you will be more likely to obtain your wish at Oakdale. Run now, and get ready, and be back before dark. Why do you not go out, Nora?"

"I spoke during study hour," answered Nora, with a deep blush.

Helen had got as far as the door, when these words arrested her. Should she too, go back? She stood a moment irresolute,—only a moment, and then she walked back and sat down by Nora. Mrs. Neville looked surprised, but said nothing.

All disappointment, however, must have an end, and at length Helen was fairly on the road to Mr. Nelson's. The air was keen and bracing; the gardens were bright with marigolds, dahlias, and scarlet sage; the changing leaves dropped at her feet, and as Helen MacGregor tripped lightly along, she thought there never was a happier girl than she.

Helen was going on in this happy way, when she saw Mary Rellim coming towards her. She looked at her admiringly, for Helen had not lost her old taste for dress, although now it was only a

secondary consideration with her. Since Barbara's
birth-day, Mary and Helen had been very good
friends, until the last few weeks. Helen had
noticed that Mary now never spoke to her when
she came to the cottage, unless to answer some
question, which she did in the shortest possible
manner. It worried Helen somewhat, and she
strove to speak kindly and if possible to overcome
Mary's dislike. She therefore greeted her very
cordially, but received only a cold return. Mary
knew at once that Helen must be going to Mr.
Nelson's, as she was so near there, and that gave
an additional haughtiness to her brow; for it was
the great point of Helen's offending that she had
found favor at Oakdale. Mary had lived all her
life in Brookfield, and had never been inside, even,
of the grounds; and yet, here was Helen, almost a
stranger, so intimate there. Mary had only heard
a few weeks before of Helen's sprained ankle; and
she now glanced at her own handsome dress and
then at Helen's common delaine, and curled her
lip to think what poor taste the master of Oakdale
had. Poor Mary! Poor even in her riches.
She was growing up with no thought beyond
dress. Her mind was occupied entirely with

20 *

dreams of coming parties and gaieties, the last new style of bonnets, and the gossip of the village. What vain pursuits to occupy an immortal soul! No working for the Master; no self-denial for that holy cause which brought a God from heaven.

"Are all well at home?" asked Helen kindly.

"Yes, very well, thank you. I suppose you are going to Oakdale?"

"Yes, and I must hurry too; it gets dark so soon now."

"Oh, you need not hurry there now, for Mr. Nelson is out."

"Out?" exclaimed Helen, in a disappointed tone, "I am so sorry. But then perhaps he will not be gone long, and I may see him yet."

"You need not go," said Mary coldly, "he will not be back while you wait."

"How do you know?" asked Helen incredulously. "I believe he will come, for he never stays out late; so I'll try."

Helen was starting off, but Mary caught her arm.

"If you will persist in going, then I must tell you that he went out because you were coming!"

"Went out because I was coming!" exclaimed Helen amazed, "who told him I was coming?"— then she added instantly, "I suppose Mrs. Neville must have told him this morning."

"Yes, to be sure," said Mary, "so, come go back with me."

"No, not now," said Helen.

"Why, you are not going down there, are you?"

"No," said Helen sadly.

"Well, then, come with me."

But all Mary's coaxing could not move Helen, and she was obliged reluctantly to let her go. Helen longed to be alone. She ran on until she reached the little woods, and throwing herself on the ground she burst into a passionate fit of weeping. Who does not know how bitter it is to be deceived for the first time? So disagreeable is the truth that we long not to believe it. Helen had, unconsciously, accorded to Mr. Nelson every virtue. So truly moral was his character, that she was apt to forget he was not a Christian; and to think that this wealthy gentleman should not be willing to lose the rent of Lucy's poor cottage when it was for such an object! For she felt convinced that Mr. Nelson had gone out to avoid a refusal. Generosity was one of Helen's good traits. She would give away the last mouthful she had to eat, or the last precious thing she possessed, to gratify another. No other fault, perhaps, would have so raised her indignation. No, not her indignation; it was not anger that Helen felt, but keen and bitter disappointment. She had raised Mr. Nelson on a pedestal in her imagination, and endowed him with all good qualities, and it cut her to the heart to think that this refined gentleman was callous to the wants of the poor. Then came some tears for the disappointment of poor Lucy. And what was to become of the five little ones through the long cold winter? Helen's old wish for wealth came back again. "Yes," she thought, "I would know how to use it better now, on the poor and the sick. But I have not got it, and wishing does not help poor Lucy. I must do all I can without it. All I can! What can I do? I can ask him. Yes, I *will* ask him. Let him refuse, I can coax; and perhaps he does not know just how poor they are. No, I don't believe he ever thought about it. Anyhow, I will do my part," and jumping up, she started off at a brisk pace. "I can wait. Poor little children, they must have a home. But," she thought, suddenly stopping, "God can do everything. I will go back and ask him for wisdom and guidance." She hastily ran back to the woods, and kneeling on the soft green moss, asked the aid and blessing of the loving Saviour, who bids us come to him in every time of need. Helen felt reassured and comforted; and stopping no more she soon reached Oakdale. She was surprised when the servant told her to walk at once into the library, as Mr. Nelson was there. She had expected to wait for him, and this sudden meeting took away all her courage. It was one thing to resolve boldly, off in the woods, quite another to execute when the time came. The spacious hall and pompous waiter struck a chill to her heart, and seemed to accuse her of presumption; a young insignificant stranger, thinking to influence the master of Oakdale! But Helen had no time to think much; the study door was thrown open and Mr. Nelson advanced to meet her. She was a little surprised at her cordial reception, but having once doubted, she thought with a pang, "Is it possible he is hypocritical too?"

She took the offered seat, and said yes and no to Mr. Nelson's questions; but at length being unable to think of any favorable beginning, she introduced the subject at once, by saying timidly,

" I know you do not wish to see me, Mr. Nelson, but,"—

" Do not wish to see you, child?" said that gentleman, in surprise, " I am always glad to see you. I would like to keep that merry face always at Oakdale."

" Well, then," said Helen, " I mean,—I mean, you do not like the errand that has brought me here."

" Why, really, Helen," said Mr. Nelson laughing, " I shall begin to think some of your own fairies have carried off your senses."

" Oh, then," said Helen, looking up with a bright smile and feeling much relieved, " then you do not mind my asking you?"

" I think it likely I can answer that question much better when I know what you are going to ask."

" Why don't you know?" asked Helen, looking puzzled; " ah, then, perhaps it was because you did not wish to see me that you went out, and not because of my errand."

"Well, well, Helen, I think there must be some grand mistake here. I have not been out since this morning, I assure you, and I did not know you were coming. Have some of the servants been denying you admittance?"

"Oh, no, not at all; I have just come."

She stopped. She could scarcely bring herself to believe that Mary Rellim had deceived her so causelessly; and she wondered what her motive could have been. But she did not think long. Mr. Nelson was anxious to know what was the matter. Helen generously refused to tell him who had deceived her, but very much encouraged, began her petition in Lucy's behalf. Helen, when excited by a subject, usually spoke with the eloquence which is native to the Highlanders, and which often astonishes strangers. She pleaded for the lonely orphans with impassioned earnestness; and Mr. Nelson allowed her to go on, without giving any signs of approval. He loved to hear that pleading young voice, and when Helen reverently said that God would surely bless him for it, no sneer curled his lip, but he bowed his head in silence before the pure trust of her childish faith.

Helen waited for an answer. She had told him of Lucy, so kind and motherly; of all the endearing ways of the little ones, down to roguish Tom and the baby; and she waited almost breathless for the result. But Mr. Nelson seemed in no hurry. He sat thinking for some time; at length looking up, he said abruptly, "Helen, I once knew a lady who, whenever there was to be any deed of charity done, went round and collected money from different parties, and then sending it in, in her name, as collected by her, she received all the credit, and was not obliged to contribute herself. Now what do you think of that?"

Helen smiled. "I think she ought to have some credit for the trouble she took in collecting, but I think she ought to have given something herself, if she could afford to."

"Exactly. I think so too. Now, if I give this cottage rent-free, for a year, what is Helen going to give?"

"I cannot give much," said Helen; "you know I am poor; but I have given all I can."

"Come, come, Miss Helen; I do not call that

fair. If you know my almsgiving so well, I think I have a right to know yours."

Helen blushed deeply. How could she tell him of the silk dresses? It would seem like such a trifling thing to him. But Mr. Nelson insisted. He felt a strong curiosity to know if this young girl was as truly generous as she appeared; and Helen, finding that she could in no other way gain her wish, told the simple story of the silk dresses, giving Nora and Barbara an equal share of praise.

What was it in that little act of true charity that called unwonted moisture to the eyes of the master of Oakdale? Perhaps it was the recollection of an unbounded wealth, that never yet had fed the hungry or cheered the desolate.

The short autumn day was drawing to a close, and Helen rose to go. Mr. Nelson put his hands on her shoulders, and looking kindly down into the upturned face, said,

"It is all right, Helen; I give Lucy the cottage for two years; and be sure and buy that wonderful baby some shoes with this;" and he put a five dollar note into her hand.

Helen thanked him warmly. Her full heart went up in gratitude to God for all his blessings.

21   Q

She hardly knew how she got home. She scarcely walked a step of the way, and on reaching the door burst into the kitchen where Mrs. Neville was preparing flannel cakes for supper, and Nora was setting the table, almost breathless with running and excited joy.

Certainly the home scene had been a very pleasant one before; the fire-light shining on the white dishes and bright tins, contrasting with the gathering twilight of a cool fall evening; but it seemed more cheerful still, now, as Helen joyfully, and almost hysterically, recounted what she called "her adventures;" while Barbara laid aside her book to listen, and Nora would pause, plate in hand, to express her admiration of the five dollars, while their merry laughter drowned the pleasant sound of the baking cakes.

Yes, no home can be happier than that which is blessed by God, and whose pleasure springs from doing good.

Laugh on, young cheerful hearts! Ye are learning the pleasure that self-sacrifice alone can give.

XVII.

THE LITTLE SCHOOL.

"Be good, sweet child, and let who will be clever;
　Do noble things, not dream them, all day long;
　So shalt thou make life, death, and that vast forever,
　One grand, sweet song."

"NOW, Tommy, you must hold still and get your hair combed," said Lucy Dean to her refractory little brother who persisted in turning his head first one side, and then the other; "Miss Helen will be here directly, and you couldn't half learn your lessons with such rumpled hair."

"Yes I could, too; I could learn just as fast."

"Oh, Tommy, what a naughty way to talk; even if you could learn just as fast, Miss Helen would not like to teach you, and what would you do then?"

"Do!" said the little fellow, with a great flourish of his arms that knocked the brush out of Lucy's hand, "why I'd play."

"Why, Tommy, ain't you ashamed? What

will you be when you grow up, if you don't learn now?"

"I'll be a dunce," answered Tommy, nothing daunted.

All the children laughed, but Tommy persisted in refusing to get ready for school; so Lucy, after a great deal of exertion, succeeded in getting him into the next room, and at once locked him in. There he kicked and screamed, and Lucy gave a weary sigh; she was at times almost tempted to give up in despair, especially when Tommy got one of his stubborn fits. But Lucy Dean did not rely on her own strength, and the cloud soon vanished from her brow. Her greatest earthly joy was the friendship of Helen MacGregor. These two girls, so different—Lucy so calm and quiet, Helen so ardent and impulsive—yet cherished for each other a warm regard. The most love was certainly on Lucy's side, for Helen was Lucy's dearest friend; and Helen had already given the first place in her friendship to Nora,—Nora so warm-hearted and so true, always so ready to help and to sympathize. Together they had commenced teaching the little Deans, for Lucy could not afford to pay for their schooling, and there were no free schools in Brookfield. One hour every afternoon these girls gave up of their leisure time; and it was no small sacrifice, for the days were getting short, and Christmas holidays were drawing near, when they wanted all their spare time to prepare presents. Lucy was just hooking Laura's dress, when some one knocked at the door.

"Why they've come too soon," said Susie, taking an admiring look in the glass before she opened the door.

Lucy started forward with a joyful face; but it was not Helen. Mary Rellim came in. Some will wonder what took Mary to Lucy's humble cottage; and yet, strange to say, she was quite a frequent visitor there. Love of admiration was one of Mary Rellim's great failings, and she received the most undisguised admiration from the simple children of the cottage. She loved to have them gather around and praise her velvet hat and silk dress. It was delightful to the vain girl to have Laura long for such a lovely bracelet, or to drink in Susie's flattering encomiums on her rosy cheeks and white hands. Mary was dressed in her new fall clothes, and she had come to be admired; so she felt rather disappointed at Lucy's

21 *

saying, "I thought it was Helen," and that Susie, instead of lingering by her side, as usual, sat down in one corner and began studying diligently. Laura was arranging some chairs, and Tom and Aleck were absent.

"Are you going to take a walk, Mary?" asked Lucy, as, having quieted the baby with some playthings, she brought out her work and began to sew.

"No, I only came round here a while. Do you expect company?" she asked, as she glanced at the arranged chairs, and Laura's neatly braided hair.

"Only Helen and Nora," said Lucy.

"Oh," said Mary, with some scorn, "they are such strangers, I suppose, that you have to make a fuss over them."

"Not much of strangers," said Susie, laughing; "why don't you know they come here every day to teach us? Helen calls this her little school."

Mary looked surprised; she knew that Helen had joined the church, but she would not have given her credit for a sacrifice which seemed enormous to her ease-loving disposition.

"I expect then she is quite a friend of yours, Miss Susie?"

"Oh, I do love her dearly, she is so sweet."

"I like Nora the best," said Laura; "but our Tom will not mind Nora, because she laughs when he says anything funny."

"I met Helen the other day going to Oakdale," said Mary.

"Yes," said Lucy, "she is a great favorite there, and I don't wonder."

"No, I don't wonder either," answered Mary; "any body who can flatter and cozen round, will be liked by Mr. Nelson, ma says. Why, would you believe it, she is always running there. The other day, when I met her, it was getting quite dark, and I don't doubt that she went there to get invited to tea."

"Oh, Mary," said Lucy indignantly, "how can you talk so? I know she very seldom goes there; and the other afternoon she went for me."

"For you!" said Mary scornfully, "so you too are a great friend of his, I suppose."

"Yes," answered Lucy with dignity, "I am a great friend of his, although I have never spoken to him; a great friend of his, because he has given me this cottage, rent free, for two years. And he did it because Helen, noble and generous as she is,

asked him to do it; and I heard old Wilkins the
gardener say that he would never have done it for
any one else. And never," continued Lucy, as the
tears started to her eyes, "never say anything to
me against Helen MacGregor, for I love her, and
I will not listen to it."

All looked amazed to see the usually quiet Lucy
thus aroused, and Mary opened her lips to reply,
when she was interrupted by a knock at the door,
and Helen and Nora entered. Nora looked slightly
annoyed when she saw Mary sitting there; for although she, as well as Helen, intended becoming a
teacher, yet she did not wish her first attempts at
teaching the multiplication table to such a refractory pupil as Tommy, commented upon by so severe a critic; but seeing that Helen did not seem
to mind it, she too welcomed Mary cordially, and
seconded Helen's invitation to stay and see the
school exercises.

Mary, hardened as she was, could not help
blushing when she spoke to Helen; but Helen
seemed so utterly unconscious, and treated her so
kindly, that Mary came to the conclusion that she
had not suspected her ungenerous conduct, and felt
very much relieved. She soon became greatly

"In bounds Helen dressed as a Highland maid." p. 205.

interested. Aleck came in just in time, and Tom
was brought from his prison in the back room,
where he had employed his time in looking
through the key-hole. Lucy had whispered to
Helen the cause of Tommy's punishment, with the
pathetic appeal,

"Do, dear Helen, do something with him; I
can not manage him at all."

Tom took his seat in the class with a rather
downcast air, and turned very red, when Helen
said gravely,

"Have you just got up, Tommy?"

"No, ma'am."

"Oh, then I expect you have not looked at
your hair yet; or have you forgotten to brush it?
Come here, I must brush it for you."

Tommy made some show of rebellion, but Helen
seemed so resolute, he thought best to submit.

"Now, Tommy, I must tell you," said Helen,
"that every time you come in school with your
hair unbrushed, I shall brush it for you."

Tommy walked to his seat with downcast eyes,
and did not see the laughing looks that were directed towards him, as he sat down entirely unconscious that his hair was parted in the middle!

Helen had already gone when he discovered it, or I am afraid she would have had rather an unruly scholar.

Helen taught Aleck and Tommy their a-b, abs, while Nora heard Laura and Susie spell. Then they exchanged classes, and Helen gave the girls addition sums on their slates, while Nora taught the boys the multiplication table; then the last quarter of an hour was devoted to attempts at reading; each being ambitious to learn to read the best and soonest. This rivalry was principally between Laura and Susie; Laura was a year the elder, but Susie was the smarter of the two, and indeed, perhaps, the brightest of the children. Tommy's barberizing had detained them a little, so that Susie, looking uneasily at the clock said,

"Indeed, Helen, if Laura don't read faster, I shall not get to read."

"Wouldn't it do, if I were to hear her this once, Helen?" asked Mary timidly.

She had looked on with an interest entirely new to her, and longed to take part. Susie pouted a little, but Helen said kindly,

"Oh, if you only would, Mary, I should be so much obliged."

Mary had a real talent for teaching, undiscovered and unknown to herself until that afternoon; both teacher and pupil became so interested in the pronunciation of hard words, that they continued the lesson after school was dismissed.

"How I like you for a reading teacher," said Susie, looking up into Mary's face.

Mary felt pleased. Perhaps for the first time in her life the spoiled child of fortune had tried to please another; and so she answered laughingly,

"And I do love to teach; I never tried it before."

"I guess you would soon get tired of it," said Lucy; "lessons do not always go as smoothly as that did; I know a little girl that sometimes pouts, and does not want to learn."

Susie smiled and looked shyly at Helen; and then running up, and putting her arms around her, she said coaxingly,

"You do not get tired of me, do you, Helen?"

"No, not yet, at least," answered Helen.

"I do not think I should ever tire of teaching," said Mary.

Helen looked at her; she saw that she was pleased and interested, and the thought instantly crossed her mind, that perhaps, if they could get Mary to take part in this simple work, it might lead her on to higher good; so she said smilingly,

" I wish I had another assistant teacher; I think we could then introduce writing in the *higher* classes. Would you like to aid us ?"

" Oh, I should love to come," said Mary eagerly, all her jealousy and ill feeling gone in prospect of the pleasure of this new employment. Helen paused thoughtfully a moment, and then said,

" You will not think hard of it, Mary, if I say that we must have punctual teachers ?"

Mary looked a little haughty at this assumption of principalship, but Nora hastened to say,

" Why, you know, Mary, it would put all our lessons out of order the days you would stay away; and we would not know what to depend on."

" Yes, so it would," said Mary frankly. " I will come punctually."

Helen thanked her for her kind offer of assistance, which would be really valuable to them, and then began to arrange for the next day's school. Helen gave Susie to Mary to teach, knowing that she was the smartest, and therefore would reflect the most credit on her teacher, and to encourage Mary in her first efforts at self-denial.

This was the starting point of Mary Rellim's improvement. Lucy prophesied that she would be tired in a week; and Mrs. Neville shook her head gravely; but Nora and Helen were hopeful, and they were not disappointed. Mary had a natural gift for teaching; she felt that she did it well, and "we all like to do what we know we do well." Her old jealousy of Helen began to disappear. Unconsciously she learned to admire and to imitate the Christian life of the two girls, with whom she was now thrown in daily intercourse. They did not talk much in school hours, but there was the long walk home together after school, for Lucy lived a little out of the village.

It is impossible for people to be brought constantly into each other's society without the stronger influencing the weaker, and Mary Rellim soon learned that Helen and Nora never gossipped, and that she must not sneer at goodness in their presence. They always had many other things to talk of, besides dress, and Mary soon found herself getting into the same habits.

Oh, the blessed power of good influence! Who

22

can reckon up the thousands it has saved from everlasting death? Mrs. Rellim had never troubled herself much about her children, so that they behaved genteelly, and kept out of mischief; but the fondest mother could not have chosen for her child better companions; and many an evening did Mary sit in the cottage planning over with her youthful companions new schemes of improvement in the little school. And then, she too would kneel with them in the evening worship.

> "The massive gates of circumstance
> Are turned upon the smallest hinge;
> And thus some seeming pettiest chance
> Oft gives our life its after tinge."

Thus Mary's visit to the orphans' cottage was overruled, in God's mercy, to her eternal good. It was her first step in the path towards the narrow road.

XVIII.

WINTER.

"We know 'tis good old winter should come,
  Roving awhile from his Lapland home;
  'Tis fitting that we should hear the sound
  Of his reindeer sledge on the slippery ground."

MONTHS fly past on joy-tipped wings when each hour brings its appropriate work and leaves it well performed. Oh, happy industry! Those alone who have learned thy pleasant ways know how much happiness earth has for them. Oh, how pitiable the lot of those children who are brought up to do nothing! They carry the misery of idleness with them through long years, to throw a pall of discontent over all the fair things of life.

The young girls of the cottage enjoyed their play hours with all the sweeter zest, because they could think with such lively satisfaction of neatly mended clothes, of an orderly household, of the hours given to faithful study, and to "heaven-

255

born charity." The autumn had passed away, and left the memory of its many treasures and pleasures richly enjoyed. Study and work had both been pursued with greater ardor as the cool weather advanced, and began to reinvigorate their systems. Home too, seemed dearer to the girls as the chilly evenings made them welcome the closed windows and cheerful fire. In summer time our homes may be pleasant, but they lack the cosy comfort of the fire-side. The little school had made good progress. Writing had been introduced, and reading had become a pleasure. The refractory had been reduced to good order, and the teachers had learned to take the warmest interest in the improvement of their little scholars. They had had their long delightful walks in the lovely sunshine of Indian summer, when they gathered the last relics of earth's decaying splendor, the brilliant leaves of the forest, or the last hardy flowers of fall; when they watched the squirrels in the almost uncovered woods, and trod with rustling step amidst the thick dead leaves. Then there had been the storing away of hickory-nuts and apples for the long winter evenings; and the chestnuting times when Nora would come in exclaiming that she had "never enjoyed such a day in her life." The autumn had indeed been a very happy one. But now old white-headed winter had assumed his authority and brought along with him the usual amount of sleigh-riding and snow-balling. It was only two weeks from Christmas, and the sewing hours for all that time were to be given up to the making of presents.

The short December day was waning. Helen, Barbara, and Nora, each drew their chairs closer to the window to take advantage of the few remaining moments of daylight, and conversed in very low tones, so as not to disturb Mrs. Neville who was writing at another window. There seemed to be an unwonted sadness over the little group; and Nora every now and then would stoop over and kiss Helen's cheek, saying, in a half mirthful, half sad tone,

"I am going to take as many kisses now as I can get, while I have you here."

And Helen would laughingly reply that she had not gone yet. Yes; a change was brooding over the happy inmates of the cottage. They were to separate. But we will read Mrs. Neville's letter for an explanation.

22 *   R

It ran thus:

DEAR SISTER STELLA,—You will wonder, I dare say, at my writing this letter ere I receive an answer to my last, knowing that I am such a poor correspondent. Do not be at all alarmed though; there is nothing serious the matter, neither have I received, what you remember in my school girl days I was always wishing for, the pen of Madame de Sévigné. No; I simply want what Sheridan once called the worst of all vices, advice. And therefore I come to you, my more than sister, for did you not through long years give me a mother's love and care? So as you have spoiled your sister by making her depend so much on you, you must go on through life, still bearing the burden of her troubles, and still advising.

You do not know our Helen, excepting, that is, by letter. You have heard who she is, how she came to be with us, and how we all have learned to love her. Her happy, generous disposition you cannot appreciate without living with her. She has endeared herself to us all, and to part with her would be a keen sorrow; but you know we are not wealthy, and Helen, like my own dear girls, must expect to earn her own livelihood when she is old enough to teach, that is, if she remains with me. But a home of wealth, a life of ease, has been offered to our Scotch girl. You remember Mr. Nelson, our rich, eccentric landlord? From the very first he took a strong liking to Helen, and he now wishes to adopt her as his own daughter. The dear child cannot bear to think of leaving us, but she has left the matter entirely in my hands. The question is, what ought I to say? Mr. Nelson is a perfect gentleman, upright and moral, but alas! he is not a Christian. Helen thinks a great deal of him. May there not be danger that he will lead her young feet out of the narrow way, into the deep waters of his own cold skepticism? And yet, on the other hand, ought I to deprive Helen of the comfort and advantages that wealth gives? She is to receive, if she goes there, every opportunity of a liberal education. And then too, I sometimes wonder if God may not be sending her there for his own good purposes, perhaps even to lead the master of Oakdale, by the example of her simple faith, to the foot of the cross. For is it not written "out of the mouth of babes and sucklings thou hast perfected praise?" And may she not one day teach him that wealth is a sacred trust, to be used in helping the poor and in spreading the glad tidings of salvation? Six months ago I should have answered unhesitatingly, no; but Helen has since then learned to care little for earthly treasures; she has found the priceless pearl; and each day seems to add to her Christian firmness and spiritual growth. Nora and Barbara are quite disconsolate at the idea of losing their companion. What shall I do? But you cannot judge well without knowing Helen. Come, then, and pay us that long promised visit. Do come. Mind, I will take no refusal. Tell father he must go over to Edith's, and stay till you come back; I know it is useless to ask him to come so far in this cold weather.

Nora and Barbara send grandpa and aunt Edith and cousin Stella a great deal of love; they will not send aunt Stella any, as they expect to see her soon, and give it to her fresh from their rosy lips. December sunlight tarries such a little while, I can scarcely see to finish this. Come soon, and give our cottage the sunshine of aunt Stella's smile. With much love,

Your affectionate sister

REBECCA.

Two weeks passed away without bringing a reply to this letter, either in the shape of aunt Stella, or her hand-writing. Mr. Nelson waited impatiently for the answer Mrs. Neville delayed to give. In the meantime, he showed special kindliness of feeling towards Helen and the girls, appreciating their tender relationship, and desiring if possible to reconcile Helen the more readily to the proposed change, if it should be finally agreed upon. Thus the day before Christmas he drove up to Mrs. Neville's door in a fine sleigh with prancing horses and ringing silver bells, to take the whole party sleigh-riding. Mrs. Neville declined going, but the three girls were in high glee, and enjoyed the ride as only girlhood can. They took supper at a hotel in the next village some ten miles off, and returned by brilliant moonlight. Just as the party reached home, and before the sleigh had fairly stopped, Nora exclaimed,

"Oh, aunt Stella has come! Aunt Stella has come! I'm certain. Didn't you see the man just come out of the gate? he has been taking in her trunk," and barely giving Mr. Nelson time to lift her out she ran towards the house. Barbara followed swiftly, and Mr. Nelson, holding Helen a moment whispered,

"Do not let them decide against me, my child."

Helen said nothing; but for the first time she wished to go to Oakdale. The solitary life of its master rose before her, cheered by no loving voice; not even solaced by the Saviour's love, or the joy that religion sheds over the most desolate surroundings.

"After all," she thought, as she walked slowly up the garden path, "we are not to do just what we like best in this world. Mr. Ashton used to say that each had a life-work; perhaps this is mine, and I will try and not shrink from it. Surely, living an easy life, in a handsome home, can be no hard lot. I remember well the time when I would not have hesitated. But then I did not know the Nevilles. Kind, motherly Mrs. Neville; dear, studious, quiet, Barbara, and darling, lovely Nora! I almost hope they will say no."

Helen lingered a few minutes, enjoying the beautiful night. She almost dreaded to go in; she had heard so much about this favorite aunt, that she rather feared to meet her. She could remain outside, no longer, however, for Nora came in search of her; and taking her in, with her arm around her, she said,

"This is our sister Helen, auntie, and you are to decide that she shall not go away from us."

Helen felt the warm lingering kiss and heard a sweet voice say, "another niece to be loved," and looking up into the kindly face above her, she felt that Nora's extravagant praise of her aunt had not been too freely bestowed.

Miss Stella Ashton was past middle age, but she looked much younger. "The peace of God which passeth all understanding," dwelt in her heart, and shed its hallowing light over her whole countenance. Her hair was black and glossy, and her dark eye had lost none of its youthful brilliancy. The mouth was firm, and spoke of duty fulfilled at all hazards; but the genial smile so seldom left the lip, that this was scarcely noticed. It was, as Nora always said, "aunt Stella's own smile."

"But how did you know I was here?" asked aunt Stella, after their bonnets and cloaks had been laid aside, and the merry group had gathered round the fire.

"Just as if we didn't know you would come on Christmas eve, like a Christmas present!" said Nora, archly.

"You must have had something more certain to judge by than the whimsical notions of this little head," said aunt Stella, giving Nora's short curls some caressing pulls.

"Yes," said Barbara, "we saw the man come out who brought your trunk."

"I do not think you saw so much as that, my dear, for my trunk is still at the depot."

"Still at the depot!" repeated Barbara, astonished.

"But we certainly saw a man come out," said Helen.

"I think it very likely you did," said Mrs. Neville smiling, "for there certainly was a man here."

"Now, mother," said Nora laughing, "I know you just want to make us curious; and I am not going to ask any questions, to show my curiosity, but I shall just run out in the kitchen and take a look round."

Barbara and Helen followed her and they soon returned, carrying a small box on which was written, "For the three bonny lasses of the cottage, Christmas, 185—." It was from Oakdale, as they had expected, and contained three handsome silk dresses.

Mr. Nelson it seemed, had not forgotten the

history of their first silks. Now, indeed, they felt
that their slight self-sacrifice had been more than
repaid. Their spontaneous expression was one of
sincerest thankfulness to their kind and generous
friend. The box also contained a short note for
Mrs. Neville, begging her to let the girls receive
the dresses as a token of the sincere admiration
with which he had heard of their ready sacrifice
of self. Mrs. Neville allowed them to keep the
dresses, but she did not show them the note.

Christmas day was very happily spent. Love
tokens were continually coming and going. Lucy
and her little flock were not forgotten in the general rejoicing. Two or three warm dresses with
turkey and mince pies found their way from Mrs.
Neville's cottage to Lucy's. Aunt Stella's presence added another charm to Christmas; and
when her trunk arrived in the afternoon, and
grandpa's presents as well as her own were dis-
tributed, pleasure reigned supreme. Each one
sank to sleep that night with a prayer of thanksgiving on her lips to that God, who to the manifold gifts of our daily life added the yet greater
gift of his only Son.

XIX.

"It is not much the world can give
    With all its subtle art,
And gold and gems are not the things
    To satisfy the heart;
But oh, if those who cluster round
    The altar and the hearth,
Have gentle words and loving smiles,
    How beautiful is earth!"

EIGHTEEN months had passed away, and
lovely June, the crown of summer, smiled in
beauty over hill and dale. The warm sunshine
lit into beauty the grand old oaks and bent the
fair heads of the myriad flowers around the white
stone house; and Oakdale looked very lovely.

The hall door opened, and Helen ran lightly
down the broad marble steps and through the long
avenue, then looked anxiously down the road.
The same Helen as of yore, only a little taller and
more womanly. But her eye still had its trusting
look, her long dark curls still floated free, only

23   265

bound to the head by a scarlet ribbon. The delicate folds of a white India muslin, which touched
the ground, made her look rather taller than she
really was.

"I wonder why they do not come?" she exclaimed a little impatiently; "it is quarter of three,
and I shall give Nora a good scolding; I told her
to be here at half-past two, and to think I sent the
carriage so as to hurry them!" And Helen
turned away, and began walking up and down the
stately avenue whose thick trees only admitted the
sunlight in brilliant patches.

For the last sixteen months Helen had lived at
Oakdale. Many bitter tears had been shed at
parting with the dear ones at the cottage; and it
was some time before Mrs. Neville could believe
that her sister's advice was best—that Helen had
no right to shrink from the destiny that seemed
marked out for her. The three girls were almost
inconsolable at the thought of separation; and none
the less, surely, after it had been accomplished.
Nora and Barbara often looked at Helen's vacant
desk with tears and ill suppressed sighs. They
missed her everywhere, and most at the daily
tasks which she had always shared with them.

And as Mr. Nelson listened with a pleased smile to Helen's light footstep on the stair case, or her song in the hall, he rejoiced that this vision of youth had come to cheer the gloomy old house, without knowing that Helen sighed as she sang; that she never trod the marble hall, or sat down in the luxurious chair to repeat her lessons to her governess, without a yearning wish for Nora's cheerful face and comical answers, or Barbara's quiet smile. But time is a great consoler; and when sixteen months had passed away they had become used to being apart, although during that time they saw each other almost daily.

Two things Helen had insisted upon as conditions of her acceptance of Mr. Nelson's offer; and to both he had given a rather reluctant consent. The first was, that she should never be obliged to give up her little school until the children left to earn their own living; the second, which was suggested by aunt Stella, was that she should be permitted to read him a chapter in the Bible every night before retiring. Both duties had been strictly fulfilled. Thus it happened that they met so frequently, and Helen nearly always stopped at the cottage on her way back. On the afternoon now introduced, she was expecting them all there to tea. I say all, as she included Mrs. Neville and aunt Stella, who was again at the cottage on a visit. The clock struck three, and Helen gave an impatient sigh, just as the carriage rolled in at the gate.

"Oh, Nora!" she exclaimed, as they were getting out, "I think you richly deserve a good scolding. Here I have been tiring myself out, walking up and down the avenue, and wearing out my neck looking over the gate; and you said you would hurry them all off!"

"Don't, please don't scold me," said Nora laughing; "it was all aunt Stella's fault."

"Yes," said aunt Stella, "I plead guilty to the charge, and I shall expect the clemency of the court when I make my confession."

"But I warn you, Aunt Stella," said Helen merrily, "that if the excuse is not good, you shall have the severest punishment the law allows. Why, did I not put aside all lessons at twelve o'clock, and have dinner a half hour earlier, which made Mr. Nelson say, 'Helen, my child, I shall begin to be jealous of those special friends, if you do not take care?' Oh, you need not look grave, my sage Nora; it is very seldom I exercise my authority; and I generally study even to suit you."

"How is Mr. Nelson?" asked Mrs. Neville.

"He is very well, thank you; but he said he would not join us until supper time; he has something to attend to."

All this time the guests had been removing their things in Helen's own room. When they had concluded, Helen proposed going down to the dell and sewing under the trees. This was unanimously agreed to, Nora saying that it did not seem like work to her to sew out of doors.

Nothing could be lovelier than that shaded grove on that warm afternoon. The air swept through the branching oaks with refreshing coolness, and the little cascades splashed and murmured in sweet harmony with the birds' songs. They found camp stools awaiting them, and each one took out her sewing and seated herself comfortably for a social afternoon. Conversation has a rare charm when carried on intelligently and well; and busy fingers and busy tongues add wings to time. The sun was nearing the west, and sending his long crimson rays deep into the midst of the dell,

23 *

making the modest little stream blush with even greater beauty.

"How lovely it is here," said aunt Stella, gazing around. It was her first visit to Oakdale.

"Yes," said Barbara; "here is where we ate our dinners the first pic-nic we ever had together."

"Rather a small pic-nic," said Mrs. Neville, "only three persons."

"Oh, I forgot to tell you," said Helen, "that I have named this charming spot. Mr. Nelson told me to do so and then afterwards he laughed at my choosing such a gloomy name."

"Why, what did you call it?" asked Nora.

"'Cypress Dell.' Don't you see those three cypresses? And somehow, when I come here alone it does seem very gloomy."

"You must have been thinking of old funeral rites, Helen," said Mrs. Neville, "when they used cypress as their emblem of gloom."

"I was reading only the other day," said Barbara, "that the coffins containing the Egyptian mummies were nearly all made of cypress wood."

"Yes, but I suppose that was on account of its durability," said her aunt.

"Well, I never thought much about funeral customs until the other day, when Mr. Nelson began talking of them. I took it for granted nearly everybody was buried in the same general way, except in those countries where they burn the dead."

"But you certainly remember, Helen," said Nora, "when we heard Dr. Scudder tell of the Togas, who used to kill six buffaloes every time a chief died, and just as many as the family could afford, for an ordinary person's funeral? Because they thought buffaloes' blood was necessary for them in the next world."

"Yes, I remember it now, but I had not thought of it since."

"But what did Mr. Nelson say, Helen?" asked Barbara, who was always eager to hear facts and incidents.

"Why, he was telling me about the Chinese in California. You know he spent two years there. He says that when a rich Chinaman dies, the priest always goes to the house, dressed in his robes, kneels down on the pavement and prays for his departed soul; and all the time he is praying, he burns what they call josh sticks,—little sticks about a foot long made of rosin, tar, and other combustible substances."

" Does he really kneel right out on the pavement?" asked Nora.

" Yes, on the pavement; but only when they have money to pay for such a display. Then they have a grand feast at the house, and at the grave too; everybody carries something along to eat. But I think the most curious part of it is, that after the person has been buried a while they take up his bones and send them in a box to China. Every Chinaman's bones are sent back to his own country. There they keep them a while and then rebury them."

" Well I never heard anything so strange as that," said Nora.

" Not so very strange, my child," said Mrs. Neville; " they are sent out to this country by companies in China, and they must be accounted for; I suppose that is one reason why their bodies are required. But I can tell you something stranger than that. There is a nation in Asia, I cannot remember the name now, that keep small dogs to eat up their dead; and these dogs are held very sacred."

"Oh, dear!" said Barbara, with a sigh of relief, "how glad I am that I live in a country where they bury people rightly."

"Better be thankful, my dear girl, that you live in a country where the religion of Jesus teaches us how to live, so that we may have part in the first resurrection. What becomes of the body after death, matters little."

"Mother," said Barbara, "I was wondering some time ago, if, after the resurrection of Lazarus, people did not ask him a great many questions about what he saw when he was dead. Do you not think they must have done so?"

"I think it is very probable they did, for human nature was the same then as it is now; but I very much doubt if he told them, even if he had the power, as we have no record of it."

"How I should like to have seen him," said Helen. "Somehow, I think he must have been different from others, after coming to life again."

"Why, aunt Stella and I were talking about that very thing last week," said Nora, "and auntie repeated to me some verses she had written on it."

"Not on his resurrection exactly, my dear, but

on the Jewish tradition, which says, that Lazarus was never known to smile afterwards; that neither anger nor sorrow nor in fact any human passion ever afterwards ruffled his brow; but that he lived perfectly calm and serene always."

"Do repeat the verses for us, aunt Stella," said Helen eagerly.

"I will; but I must tell you, they are written in imitation of Mrs. Hemans's poem on the death of the Prince of Wales."

"HE NEVER SMILED AGAIN."

"*Come forth!*" A calm voice broke the air,
　　As sweet as music deep,
　　As thrilling as the wind-kissed harp
　　The wand'ring breezes sweep.
　　It pierced the marble ear of Death,
　　　And broke his icy chain:
　　Lazarus came forth to life and love,—
　　　But never smiled again.

"*Come forth!*" The dread of human hearts
　　Bowed to a mightier One;
　　Death yielded up his conquered crown
　　　To God's eternal Son.
　　Lazarus awoke on earth once more,
　　　To all earth's joy and pain;
　　But the voice of God had waked him,—
　　　"He never smiled again."

He met dear friends, the loved of years,
   In halls of festive mirth;
Fame's wreath,unsought for,pressed his brow;
   He turned from dreams of earth.
His eye had gazed on unknown shores,
   His heart had felt death's chain,
His lips had said farewell to life,—
   " He never smiled again."

He came from realms where spirits meet—
   Homes of the mighty dead;
He kept within his heart the charm
   Immortal joy had shed.
His soul still dwelt in that far land,
   Still heard its music's strain;
What were earth's deepest joys to him?—
   " He never smiled again."

Calm as the calmest mountain lake
   In some sequestered spot;
Pure as the stream in eastern lake,
   Which meets but mingles not;
Cold as the flash of jewels bright;
   Sad as remembered strain;
He knew earth's greatest mystery,—
   "He never smiled again."

" I should like to have been Lazarus," said
Barbara, "for he need never have been afraid to
die."

" And surely we need none of us be afraid to

die, if we, like Lazarus, have the Saviour for our friend," said Mrs. Neville.

> "'Jesus can make the dying bed
> Feel soft as downy pillows are.'"

"I am sure," said Helen, "I would like to write poetry as well as aunt Stella does. But then we cannot have everything we wish."

"And what is it Helen wishes for?" asked Mr. Nelson, coming up in time to hear the last sentence.

"Something that even you cannot give me," said Helen laughing,—"a talent for writing poetry."

"Yes, that passes my powers of giving," said he, laying his hand caressingly on Helen's head. "Now if you will allow a drone in this busy hive," he continued, "I will take a seat."

"Well, as you have sat down by me," said Nora, "I give you fair warning, you will have to thread all my needles; and I use a great many, as I am working this slipper in so many colors."

"Very well, I will try it a while, and if I get tired, I suppose I shall be permitted to change my seat! Did Helen give you the promised scolding that she threatened?"

"Not yet," said Nora laughing, "for I have Eve's propensity of throwing the blame on some one else."

"True enough," said Helen, "that just makes me think, aunt Stella, you have not made your excuses yet."

"Well then," said aunt Stella, "suppose I begin now. I went round to see your friend Lucy Dean. You know she has been trying to get a place for Laura, as she is quite a large girl now; and I thought if Lucy was willing, I would take her home with me."

"Oh, I am so glad," said Helen; "I wanted her to get a kind home, she is such a sensitive child. What did Lucy say?"

"She was very glad, although she said it would be hard to part with Laura; so I promised I would bring her with me every time I came, if it was possible. But I must confess I took a greater fancy to Susie, she seemed so quick."

"Yes," said Nora, "Susie is very nice; I do hope that she too will get some place where the people will take an interest in her."

"And give her an opportunity to improve," said Helen.

24

The conversation was here interrupted by the sound of the tea-bell, and the rising of Mr. Nelson inviting the party to the house.

"I am sorry Mary Rellim is not here," said Helen, as they were leaving the dell.

"And to think, she is a hundred miles away, and does not know we are wishing for her," said Nora. "How does she like her school?"

"Very much," answered Helen; "I got a letter from her only yesterday; I will show it to you after supper. She complains a little of having to study too hard. I do like Mary very much; she is so different from what she used to be."

"Helen," said Mr. Nelson in a low tone, as they were going up the steps together, "wouldn't *you* like to take Susie? If you would, take her, my child, by all means. I have no objection."

Helen gave him a joyous glance, and said in a subdued tone, "Thank you, father."

Mr. Nelson was more than repaid by hearing Helen's girlish voice call him father; which it so seldom did, that the charm never wore off for the solitary man. He was certainly much changed. Mrs. Neville had noticed it. He was more genial, and the sneer of unbelief which usually deformed his mouth, was now much rarer. Helen was throwing some of her own generous faith into the worldly life of her protector.

The evening was spent in pleasant amusement. Nora and Barbara played duets on the piano; and Helen played on the harp, and sang many pieces, both new and old, for she now had a singing master, and seldom played or sang the wild songs of her mountain home, unless on stormy evenings at Mr. Nelson's request, when he said they chimed with his feelings. And often when the wild sweet notes were dying away, Helen would take her little Bible, and sitting down by his side would almost whisper,

"Father dear, you are sad to-night; I will read you some consolation from the blessed Book."

And what would be the thoughts of that worldly heart, as the Saviour's divine invitations smote the ear? Did it reply, with Agrippa, "Almost thou persuadest me to be a Christian?"—or, like the rich man in the parable, "Soul, thou hast much goods laid up for many years; take thine ease?" Were the memories of childhood busy? Did the sunlight of other days picture to his recalling vision his baby form, as it knelt and lisped its first prayer? Did he hear his mother's voice urging him to come to Jesus? Helen never knew. He did not object to her reading, but he made no comment on it; and Helen, softly closing the Book, would kiss his brow, and retire to her own room to pray earnestly that God's Holy Spirit would touch that stony heart, and send it a weeping supplicant to the foot of the cross.

XX.

AN ARRIVAL.

"Whatever passes as a cloud between
   The eye of faith and things unseen,
   Causing that bright world to disappear,
   Or seem less lovely or its hopes less dear,—
   This is our world, our idol, though it wear
   Affection's impress, or devotion's air."

"IT is all right, Lucy, you need not worry about that," said Helen, as they were parting at the gate of the avenue; for Lucy had walked home with Helen after school. "Mr. Nelson told me I was to do just as I pleased about everything, and you need never speak about rent. Anyhow, the two years will not be up until October, and this is only July. Won't you come in, and see Susie?"

"No, not this afternoon; Aleck wanted me to hurry back, as he wishes to go and see the gentleman Mr. Nelson spoke to, about that place in his store. I am so much obliged to you, Helen."

"Now hush, Lucy; you *know* I will not allow that. Good-bye until to-morrow."

"Good-bye," said Lucy, turning away and giving a little sigh of regret, as she looked back at Helen's white dress disappearing among the dark trees. "She is always happy and merry," she thought, "and I am always desponding; after all, she too would perhaps lose her gay spirits in a humble cottage."

While Lucy walked slowly homewards Helen ran lightly towards the library, as she always did after even a short absence, to tell Mr. Nelson of her return, and what she had been doing. Her hand was on the door, when the waiter stepped up.

"Miss Helen, there is a gentleman in the parlor who wishes to see you."

"A gentleman wishes to see me?" said Helen looking surprised. "Are you sure he asked for me, Thomas?"

"Yes, Miss, sure. He asked if Miss MacGregor was in."

Helen went into the library to ask Mr. Nelson if he knew who it was, but Mr. Nelson was not there as usual; so thinking he might be in the parlor, she threw aside her hat and went in. Mr. Nelson was not there; but a tall gentleman rose from the sofa, and looked at Helen in some surprise. But the look only lasted an instant, for Helen bounded forward and threw her arms around his neck exclaiming, " Malcom! My brother, my brother!"

Malcom returned the caress with unusual warmth. Helen could scarcely believe it possible that it was he. She looked at him again and again, and saw the same Malcom as of old. But to Malcom, Helen was much changed. He had forgotten the lapse of years, and had always thought of her as still a child; but the lady-like, refined young maiden before him bore little resemblance to the half wild girl of their native mountains. Helen's first inquiry was after her father. He was dead. The shock almost stopped her heart's beating a moment, it was so unexpected. She shed some tears for the father she had scarcely known; but years and separation had lessened a love never deep, and Helen wept almost as she would have done for a stranger. And Donald MacGregor, sleeping far off in his native Highlands, was spared the bitter pang of knowing that the daughter of whom he was so proud, and whom he really loved, had formed dearer and happier ties, in which the memory of him and his careless indifference had alike perished.

"And old Margie," said Helen, a smile chasing away the tears, "does she still crone over the peat fire and visit the haunted dell?"

"I do not know what her peculiar habits are; I know she still lives in the old place, and is more crabbed and cross than ever."

"Oh, how can you say so, Malcom," said Helen reprovingly, "you know how kind she used to be."

"To *you*, yes; but my memory fails to recall any waste of kindness bestowed on me. However, let that pass. I ask no favors of any one; I can take care of myself," he replied with some return of his old surly manner.

Helen thought best not to argue the point, but she saw with sorrow that Malcom was still the same in disposition as when in childish fun she had nick-named him "surly Malcom."

"And Dugald, how is he?"

"Dugald who?" asked her brother.

"Oh, Malcom, you certainly remember Dugald Stuart, the blind harper."

"I know nothing about him. I have something better to do than to hunt up musical beggars," answered Malcom haughtily.

Helen gave a little sigh of disappointment; it would have been so nice to have heard from her old friend. She wondered if he were still alive, and whether he ever thought of his "mountain flower."

Helen then inquired into the mystery of the unanswered letters; it was soon explained. Shortly after Helen's departure her father had been seized with a severe illness. He would not consent to having a physician; old Margaret's simple arts were unavailing, and Donald MacGregor died, as he had lived, hugging his haughty independence, and carrying his proud, solitary spirit to the grave. Helen gave a slight shudder, as she thought that he had gone into the presence of that God who out of Christ is a consuming fire. Immediately after his father's death, Malcom went to Edinburgh, where he had remained until a couple of months before, when he made up his mind to come to America.

"But how did you find me?" asked Helen. "Did you get any of my letters?"

"Not until just before starting. I went to the

mountains to get some things I had left there, when Margaret gave me the letters which she had been hoarding up as a great treasure."

" And did you read them to her?"

" No," was the short reply.

" Poor Margaret," said Helen, "I know she would like to have heard them. You told her though that I was well and happy, did you not, Malcom?"

" Oh, yes, I gave her ample satisfaction," he said with a slight sneer.

" Dear old Margie," said Helen, with a soft smile on her lip, "she used to say I would some day come back to her a grand lady; but I do not think I will ever see her again."

" Pity she did not know you think so much of her," said her brother in a scornful tone.

A quick reply rose to Helen's lip, but she repressed it and asked how he had found her.

" I inquired at Mrs. Neville's, and they directed me here," he answered, inwardly wondering what had become of Helen's quick temper, which he had always had the unfortunate power of rousing by his sneering answers. But these now seemed lost on the self-possessed young girl before him.

Malcom glanced round the room with secret envy at Helen's better lot. He had obtained an ordinary situation in New York, and had come to Brookfield with the intention of taking Helen from the Nevilles, where, he instinctively felt, from reading the letters, they could not afford to keep her without some loss. He intended to keep house in New York, and he wanted Helen for a housekeeper. She had left the Nevilles, and when he found how she was situated, his better nature whispered to him to let her remain. But •Malcom's better nature seldom gained the day. Selfishness was his ruling trait; and no kind, parental discipline had in childhood checked the poisonous growth. It would add much to his comfort to have Helen's useful hands to tend to his house and mend his clothes. And it gratified Malcom's pride, to think that Helen's refinement and accomplishments would add to his humble home a lustre which would reflect on himself. He told her of his situation and prospects, and Helen listened with interest. But when he spoke of wishing to take a small house, so as to have a home of his own, a thrill of disappointment ran through her heart as she thought, perhaps it might be her duty to go with him and make it indeed a home. She made up her mind to think over it; but she was entirely unprepared for the selfishness which could ask it of her, almost demand it as a right. With a violent effort, she strove to hide the keen pang of pain which the question gave her, as she answered she would think of it. Think of it? She could not banish the thought. It glided along, like an undercurrent, through everything she said or listened to, for the rest of the evening.

Mr. Nelson came in and invited Malcom to make his home there, while in Brookfield. This he refused, with a hauteur that wounded Helen; but he stayed to tea, and Helen had the conviction forced upon her, that Mr. Nelson and his guest disliked each other heartily. She played and sang, and laughed gaily, to hide the cloud from Mr. Nelson's searching but kindly eye. But underneath all, the struggling questions would force themselves up, "Must I go? Must I indeed go and live with one so uncongenial? Must I leave this home of ease and refinement, my dearest studies, and my kindest friends, for one who cares little for me? For one who lacks the polish of the world, or the gentleness of goodness?

Is it thy will, O my Father?" Such were the pleading, half despairing questions, that rose continually from that young heart. She longed to be alone. Alone, to pray for strength and guidance.

Malcom left early, and Helen at once took her Bible to read, although not yet the usual hour. Mr. Nelson made no remark; he heard in the tremulous tones of the reader that her heart was stirred to its very depths. And when she bade him good-night, he clasped her in a fond embrace; an embrace that seemed, all unconscious as he was, to foreshadow by its tenderness a coming sorrow. Perhaps too, a little jealousy lurked in that fond good-night. Hitherto none had shared an equal claim with Mr. Nelson upon Helen's lot and prospects in life, and he was fast making an idol of her. Now another, and one claiming the nearer name of brother had come to take, perhaps, the first place in Helen's heart.

I sometimes wonder, if there is any sin human beings are so apt to fall into as idolatry. It is so subtle, so much less easily recognized than other sins. It is so easy to give ambition, or wealth, or some frail human creature the first place in our hearts, and God the second. Do we not uncon-

25   r

sciously find ourselves asking first whether it will please another; and afterward, whether it will please the Saviour? But, oh, tempted, erring one, bend the knee in reverent thanksgiving, that God is all merciful. The blow may be sharp and keen, but the soul turns from its shattered idol, to the worship of the true God.

XXI.

THE DECISION.

" By the thorn road, and none other,
Is the mount of vision won;
Tread it without shrinking, brother !
Jesus trod it,—press thou on !"

"IF any man will come after me, let him deny himself, and take up his cross daily, and follow me." Such were the words that fell from the lips of Him who knew the end from the beginning,—One who could trace to its most hidden depths the deepest sorrow of human passion. But his eye was omniscient, and far beyond the wearying, heavy cross of to-day, he saw the starry crown of the everlasting years that should some time press the brows of his chosen. Yes, the Son of God, who could thus command his beloved ones to take up their cross, knew that through his strength they should step forth into immortality " more than conquerors."

"For a few brief hours the cross,
For untold years the crown."

We all have been brought face to face with the great struggle between duty and inclination, and poor human nature shrinks from the contest. Who has not heard the syren whisper, enjoy the present, let the future take care of itself? Who has not felt like shutting his ears to the disagreeable calls of duty, and yielding with reckless indifference to the intoxicating pleasure of the moment? Some such idea of stifling conscience possessed Helen as she entered her room that evening, and locking her door threw herself on the bed to let thought, like a "lava tide," sweep over her. She was young, full of refined taste and feeling; she loved her guardian; she loved her companions; she liked her home of ease and pleasure; and bitter indeed did it seem to have to leave them. She would not; no, she would not; she said to herself many times. It was very selfish in Malcom to ask it. But this mood did not last. Her better nature whispered, "Will you let Christ do everything for you, while you do nothing for him? Will you let your brother go on in his sinful career, and never put forth an effort to win his soul to your Saviour? Perhaps on your going or staying may depend his eternal welfare."

Helen was startled at the thought, and yet it was all too true. Malcom knew little about religion, and cared less. Thrown among the many temptations of New York, with no shield but his own weak nature, he must sink lower and lower. Then too, he would have to board, and perhaps be brought daily in contact with those more wicked than himself. But, on the other hand, if she kept house for him, if she strove by every means in her power to make home cheerful, might he not learn to love her, and to like his humble home? And then what good, through God's blessing, her influence might do him? She might gradually win him to listen to the Bible, and to attend church with her. Then too, he was her brother, even if she had never been taught to care for him, or had never received his love; still, he was her brother, the blood of the same ancestors flowed in their veins. The picture grew almost pleasant. But the next instant it was blotted from the canvas by the sudden thought of Malcom as he really was, surly and ill-tempered; of hours of loneliness and poverty; of Nora and Barbara; of Mr. Nelson's

25 *

indulgence, and all the light and love and joy she
must forsake; and throwing herself on her knees,
she prayed with passionate earnestness for grace
and guidance. But no light seemed to dawn.
Blinded by her own wild wishes she could not see
her Saviour; and the clock had struck the midnight hour before she rose from that sorrowful
vigil. But peace was written on her brow; and
if tears still lingered on her dark eye-lashes, and
dropped on her trembling lips, she yet looked
forward into the future with a steady eye. The
struggle had been keen and bitter, but it was
over; she had been given strength to do her duty;
and she saw, as if with a gifted vision, that had
she remained where she was, she might yet have
been led astray by the fond indulgence which
would not admit that she had any faults, or the
boundless wealth entirely at her disposal. And
Helen sank to sleep saying, "Jesus knows what is
best."

She had been tossed from the green shores and
sweet air of a sunny land into rough waters. She
had tried to struggle back, but almost sinking she
had caught the hand stretched out to save. It
bore her in an opposite direction, but she yielded.

It landed her far from the sun-lit isle, on a bleak and desolate shore. She missed the loved faces of her companions, but looking up she saw the Saviour. He was with her still. He would never forsake; and even the most desolate spot became sweet, when lighted by his presence.

Days passed away. Malcom had left Brookfield after obtaining Helen's promise, and telling her he would come on for her in a few weeks, as soon as he had procured a house and furnished it. Helen still hesitated to tell Mr. Nelson her decision. She felt like putting off the dreaded day as long as possible. But she could not well hide from him that something was wrong. He missed her gay song and light laugh, and sent her off one afternoon to take tea at the cottage, thinking thus to cheer her up. Here Helen told her kind friends of her intended departure. Nora and Barbara loudly protested against it; and Nora, bursting into tears, clung to Helen as though she were that instant going. But Mrs. Neville said nothing, and Helen looked at her almost hoping she would make some objection; but no, Mrs. Neville thought it was Helen's duty to go; and she bade her comfort herself with the sure word

of promise, " All things work together for good, to
them that love God." One thing she strongly
advised, that Mr. Nelson should be told at once;
and Helen thought she would tell him on the road
home. But going home, she concluded she would
tell him when she bade him good night; and when
that moment came, she was as reluctant as ever.
But she knew that it must be done; so summoning all her courage, she hurried through the account with such breathless haste that Mr. Nelson
had scarcely realized what she had said, before she
had finished.

" Did you say you were going away in a week
or two?" he asked incredulously.

" Yes, sir," said Helen, firmly and sadly.

Mr. Nelson said no more; he rose and walked
up and down the room with hasty steps and
frowning brow. Helen waited a few minutes.
She longed to speak some words of consolation before leaving him; but coming up to her he said
abruptly,

" Remember, my daughter, I will never give
you up."

" Ah, do not say so, my father; what God wills,
who shall gainsay ?"

"You do not know what God wills," he answered impatiently; "men do as they choose, and as they like best, and then say that God wills it. Nonsense."

"Dear father," said Helen in a winning tone, "is there no such thing as duty? Does not our conscience tell us when we do right and when we do wrong?"

"But there is mistaken duty, mistaken duty, Helen."

"True," answered the girl slowly; "human nature is so full of faults, so full of fond feelings; it is such a pleasure to yield to those we love, that we are apt to persuade ourselves it is our duty, when it is only our inclination."

"Well, well, then," said he, "you are mistaken; it is your duty to stay here, and your inclination calls you away."

She shook her head with a sad smile.

"Do you suppose God would leave us without anything to depend on but our weak hearts and fond fancies? He has said of the Christian, 'he shall call upon me and I will answer him: I will be with him in trouble; I will deliver him and honor him.' Dear father, I have taken this question to Jesus to decide and I have received an answer. I must go."

Mr. Nelson said nothing; he sat down on the sofa, and covered his face with his hand. He had been a lonely man; an orphan, wealthy and proud; and his cynical disposition had led him to shun his fellow-men, as well as to sneer at religion. Helen's nature, so confidingly free and full of love, had won its way into his icy heart.

> "There's not a hearth, however rude,
> But hath some little flower
> To brighten up its solitude,
> And scent the evening hour."

Helen had become to him that flower, and now to lose her seemed but too hard. "It is only another leaf in my bitter book of life," he murmured suddenly to himself. Tears filled Helen's eyes. She sat down by him and laid her head on his shoulder.

"Leave me," he said coldly.

"Then you are angry," she said sadly, as she rose to obey.

"Angry? oh, no; anger is not the word to use to a heart stung by ingratitude."

" Ingratitude!" said Helen with a start, "Am I then ungrateful?"

" Ah, Helen, Helen, what else can you call it? I took you, and made you my daughter; all the accomplishments that wealth can give, I am giving you; you might have asked me for anything, and had it been in my power, it should have been yours. And all I asked was, that you should lighten my dull old home with your presence; that you should look up to me and love me as your father. But all this has failed to please you; one whom you scarcely know, bearing the name of brother, arrives, and you turn from me with indifference to find a new home."

" Oh, no, no, not with indifference; how can you say so? I have tried to hide how much I feel this parting; but if you think me ungrateful, I will tell you all. Know then, that it is hard for me to go; God alone knows how hard. My love for you, my second father; my liking for the beauty and refinement around me, all urge me to stay."

" Stay then; stay, Helen; why should you go? We have only a short time to live in this world; let us enjoy ourselves to the utmost."

Never had Helen before so much need of high principle and firm faith. It was the hour of her great temptation. The voice of affection was urging her to accept wealth and ease, and duty was pointing to a lonely, unloved brother whom she might reclaim. "Why should I go?" she thought. "Am I ever to be tossed from one home to another? Let me stay yet a few months, and then there will be time enough to think about it."

Mr. Nelson saw she was hesitating, and he said eagerly,

"Yes, stay, my child; life was given us to enjoy ourselves in; we shall soon sleep an eternal sleep; then let us make the most of it."

Helen started, shocked at the idea, and raising her head she said hastily,

"I thank you for that reminder. Yes, we shall soon all sleep our last sleep; but, oh, it will not be eternal. There is an awaking! There is a day of judgment. Oh, my father, there is something more to live for than pleasure. There is duty to man, and duty to God. There is a higher and holier existence than the worldly know. There is a joy even in sacrifice, when it wins the smile of our Saviour. Urge me no more; I must not,

I cannot stay; and oh, my father, yield to the blessed Jesus; learn to love him, and then you will forgive your daughter, that still loving you she could leave you."

As Helen finished speaking she hastened from the parlor to seek the solitude of her own room,—on her knees to ask that strength which is never denied. Those were bitter days for her, and she needed deep draughts from the fountain of living water. She had learned to love her adopted father with all the affectionate trust of her nature; and she had thought he would look upon her duty as she did. Upright and generous in his actions, Helen expected his aid. Ah, she was finding out that where feeling and desire are opposed to duty, religion alone can give the strength to conquer for the right. Mr. Nelson was moral and just; what the world too often calls a good man; but the one great foundation of Christ Jesus, he had never built on; and now in the testing hour, when the question of right and wrong came before him, he failed in high principle. The very foundation of his character was wrong; and all the sandy ground of his morality and pride was washed away before the tide of everlasting truth. Sorrow-

26

fully Helen thought of all this, and she did all she could for him, then she prayed. And yet, even in her sorrow, the thought came into her mind that it was best for her that it had happened as it had. She was beginning to trust Mr. Nelson too much, to consider him better than he was; and his being the stronger mind, Helen shuddered to think that he at last might have led her astray from the narrow path, instead of her leading him to the Saviour, as she had fondly hoped to do. She felt that she had been awakened by God, in his merciful providence, on the brink of a precipice; and although the disappointment was bitter, she was compelled to confess that no human character can be depended on, unless strengthened and upheld by divine grace.

The next three weeks were so gloomy that Helen almost rejoiced to see Malcom. Mr. Nelson had treated her kindly and would never listen to another word on the painful subject; but Helen felt instinctively, that something was wanting. Mr. Nelson had returned to his cold and reserved manners.

Very sad indeed, was Helen's parting with her friends at the cottage. She went all over the house, to her own little room, which still bore her name; to the study, the pleasant parlor, and the dear old kitchen, and lovely garden. Everything was remembered with keen regret. Mrs. Neville, Barbara and Nora, went with her to the railroad depot; and Lucy and her little ones came in for a share of tears and caresses.

"Never mind, Lucy," said Helen, "God is the 'Father of the fatherless.' I promised you things the other day which I cannot now give. How little we can read the future."

It was almost time to start, and Helen entered the study with a slow step; but Mr. Nelson did not hear her. He was sitting with his back to the door and his head in his hand. Helen stood close beside him, and stooping down she laid her little Bible on his lap.

"Dear father," said she, "read it for my sake, when I am gone."

He glanced up hastily, and Helen saw a tear drop on the tiny book. He folded her tenderly in his arms and kissed her cheek.

"You promise, father?" she whispered, in a voice broken by sobs.

"I promise," he replied; and in a few minutes

Helen was seated in the carriage and rolling towards the depot. Oakdale with all its attractions was fading in the distance. Helen leaned forward to catch a last glimpse of the white house and green trees and of little Brookfield where she had spent so many happy hours. And the words of the text came with strengthening power, "He that loveth father or mother more than me is not worthy of me."

XXII.

DOMESTIC LIFE.

"There are briers besetting every path,
   Which call for patient care;
There is a cross in every lot,
   And an earnest need for prayer;
But a lowly heart that leans on thee
   Is happy anywhere."

THERE is such a charm in novelty, that it was
some weeks before Helen realized what a
great change had befallen her. There was so
much to do, and everything was left to her, as
Malcom refused to hire anything done that Helen
could possibly accomplish. There were carpets to
put down, furniture to arrange, and closets to clean
and put in order. Then Malcom's clothes were
sadly out of order; there were stockings to darn,
and buttons to sew on. How thankful Helen
now was for the sewing hours at the cottage, which
she at first used to consider such a hardship. And
as she sat sewing, she often thought with regret

26 *   u   305

of the cheerful little study and its pleasant inmates, of the bright garden beyond, and the
waving trees. Here she looked out on a narrow
street, the high brick walls opposite nearly shutting out the little glimpse of blue sky. And then
the little, little yard, no garden here. She had,
however, already planted in its tiny flower bed the
seeds which she had brought from Oakdale; and
one scarlet geranium in bloom stood on the window ledge near which she sat; and ever and anon
she bent over it with a smile, for it wafted her
back to the bright spot from whence it had been
taken and where its companions still bloomed in
blushing beauty. Sadness was foreign to the
nature of Helen MacGregor; and soon the dark
house rang with her merry song, as full of glee as
when it echoed through the stately halls of Oakdale. To be sure, she had her hours of loneliness
and home-sickness; but one unfailing fountain of
comfort ever remained. At such times she took
her Bible, and read and thought, until life's
troubles were banished by sweet communion with
her Saviour. No matter what she felt, she ever
strove to have her happiest smiles and most cheerful words ready for Malcom when he came home.

She led a very quiet life. Malcom went away at half past six in the morning, and took his dinner with him, as it was too far for him to return at noon, and he did not get back until six in the evening. After doing up the household work, Helen usually sewed and read in the morning, and took a walk in the afternoon. She knew no one, and these solitary walks were her only amusement. She enjoyed them very much. At first she had only gone short distances for fear of losing her way, but gradually she went farther and farther, until some evenings she had almost to run in order to reach home in time to get Malcom's supper, as he always insisted on having it ready as soon as he came in. Helen's great delight in these walks was to look in the store windows. Of this she thought she would never tire. Brought up in the country all her life, it was almost enchantment to her to see the long rows of splendid windows with all their glittering treasures. One afternoon she had been lost in admiration in front of a picture store, where the exquisite engravings and colored prints had quite made her forget how time was going, until a clock in the neighborhood warned her she should be at home. She hurried back through the crowded streets, scarcely conscious of the jostling she received, for her mind still lingered amidst the lovely Italian scenes she had been looking at.

"Half past five!" she exclaimed, as she threw open the shutters of the room that served them for parlor, dining-room, and kitchen; "now I must hurry."

She put on the coffee, and turning round, she uttered an exclamation of joy; there lay a letter on the floor, and from Nora too, she knew the hand-writing. The postman finding no one at home, had slipped it under the door. Helen kissed it, and said with a resigned air,

"I must not read it now, I must get supper first."

She bustled about, cut the bread, put the meat on to fry, for as Malcom did not come home to dinner, he always wanted a hot supper. But the more Helen hurried, the more it seemed to put her back, and at length stopping in the middle of the room, she burst into a merry laugh. "Well, I won't hurry any more," she said, "I went and brought the butter out of the cellar, and put it into the closet, instead of on the table. What is the difference, whether I read my letter now, or after supper? I can be anticipating the pleasure all through supper time, and thus get twice as much enjoyment out of it."

Just then some one knocked, and Helen opened the door. Two ragged little children stood there.

"Will you please give me a piece of bread, ma'am?" asked the oldest girl.

"Poor children," said Helen compassionately, as she glanced at their bare feet and ragged clothes, "Come in and I will get you something. Cannot your father and mother get bread for you?" she continued, as she commenced spreading each one a large slice of bread.

"Father's dead," answered the girl, "and mother's got six children, and she can't get no work."

"Poor children! Why, how do you live?"

"We mostly starves, when we can't get nothing to eat," answered the girl.

"How dreadful," said Helen, "I will get you some meat."

Helen had only intended giving the bread, but this tale of destitution awoke all her generous nature. She would give them all she could, she thought, and ask them where they lived, and perhaps she could find them out and help them occasionally. Helen ran down into the cellar to get the meat. "Oh, dear," she sighed, as she glanced at the almost empty safe, "it is so little, it won't go far for six hungry children and their mother. If I were at Oakdale now, what a plentiful supper they could get, there is so much wasted there; but I must do the best I can."

She ran up stairs with the cold meat, but the children had disappeared. She looked out of the open door, they were not in sight, but at that moment Malcom stepped up, and Helen turned quickly to the half finished supper.

"Looking for me?" asked Malcom gruffly.

"No," said Helen.

"Well, what's the matter then, supper not ready, and you standing staring round?"

"Oh, what shall I do?" said Helen, "they've taken that large loaf of bread, and we have not enough left for supper."

"They! Who?" asked Malcom.

"Two little beggar children; I went down into the cellar to get them some meat, and when I came up they were gone."

"And you brought them in here and left them," said Malcom, leaning back in his chair and giving a loud laugh; "well, Helen, you are a green one. I dare say they have taken something else."

Helen colored deeply with mortification; and, she could scarcely keep from feeling angry at her brother's rude manner; but the Christian may seek help at all times; and even a sigh for strength to overcome, for Christ's sake, reaches the divine ear. Helen soon recovered her spirits and joined in the laugh. But Malcom laughed no more.

"Remember, Helen," he said sternly, "I'll have no more feeding beggars, whether they're honest or not. I have enough to do to provide for my own wants, without supporting all the vagabond children in New York. Mind, not another piece of bread do you give away; it will take me long enough to get rich as it is, and that is all I'm living for."

Helen was greatly shocked to hear this, and she thought she would read that very evening the parable of the rich man; for Helen always would read aloud a chapter in the Bible every evening, notwithstanding Malcom's objection. Sometimes he left the room, but he generally sat in sullen silence, and she could not tell whether he listened or not. But that, and praying for him, were the only things she could do, since whenever she might make a remark which he did not wish to hear, he would cut it short with the irreverent exclamation, "None of your preaching, girl, or I'm off," and Helen, rather than send him out to roam about the streets, would keep quiet. So she said nothing, but having gone after bread, they sat down to supper.

"Oh, the spoons!" said Helen in dismay.

Yes, the two silver spoons were gone, and the only silver ones they had. Helen could hardly keep back the tears. Those two spoons had belonged to Miriam Ashton, and Mrs. Neville had given them to Helen as a keepsake; and she had never looked at them without remembering the lovely Christian woman, who slept beneath the broad Atlantic. Then too those spoons had been to Scotland, and had crossed the Atlantic with Helen. No wonder that she almost cried.

"I would rather they had taken anything else," she said.

"Don't be simple, Helen," said her brother,

"they're gone now, and 'there's no use crying over spilt milk.' Do give me some tea."

Helen got out the pewter spoons, and supper ended in silence. She had quite forgotten her letter in the mishaps of supper time; but it now brought back the smiles to her face, and chased away every gloomy feeling, as she eagerly broke it open and read,

"DEAR HELEN,—I could not tell you how glad I was to receive your long letter. Mother and Barbara both laughed at me because I kissed it so often; but I always said in answer, that your dear fingers had folded it, and that it had lived with you a while, all unconscious of its happy privilege. First I read it aloud to our folks, and just as I had finished it, Mr. Nelson came in, and he seemed so delighted to hear from you, that I read it to him. Do excuse me, dear, I will keep the next more private; but you know this was the first, and we all felt so interested, especially Mr. Nelson. He comes to our house almost every day; but although he never mentions your name, mother says he just comes to hear us talk about you, which I do nearly all the time. Mother thinks him very much changed. She was so surprised the other day, when they were talking together, to hear him say, 'I agree with you Mrs. Neville, there is no book in the world like the Bible.'"

When Helen read that sentence, she bent her head on her hand, and a prayer of thanksgiving rose to God, as she thought that through his great

27

mercy her little Bible might yet win her adopted father to the blessed Saviour. Helen read on:

" I suppose you would like to hear something about our little school. It is very small indeed now; such a falling off, both of teachers and scholars; first Mary Rellim, then Laura, then you. Now I am the only teacher, and I have but three scholars, for Aleck has a situation as errand boy in Mr. Thompson's store, and lives with him. Susie still comes, although it is a long way from Oakdale, for as you expected, Mr. Nelson asked her to stay there; he also told Lucy the cottage was hers for another year. Wasn't he kind? Lucy gets along nicely now, having only two to provide for; but she says it is very lonely without Laura and Susie at night after the little ones are in bed. She misses you very much, and sends a great deal of love. But I must tell you about my scholars. There is Tommy still; and the baby is beginning his letters, he knows O, and A; so you see my school is quite flourishing. But, oh, dear Helen, how I do miss you. Instead of getting used to it, it seems to me that every time I walk towards Lucy's cottage, I feel our separation more than ever. And indeed sometimes it is quite a task for me to go there; and then that worries me, for I get thinking that after all, perhaps when I was teaching before, I did it only because you taught, and I wanted to help you, instead of trying to please the dear Saviour. I am always so easily led away. I was so sorry to hear you had no garden, that is, none in New York; you have one here still, and I weed it regularly and water the flowers. The little rosebud I enclose, is from your favorite bush." ——

Helen smiled. Nora had forgotten to enclose it.

"Everything looks lovely, but would seem lovelier still if you were here. I have not been at Oakdale since you left; I am waiting until you come back; for I have the bump of hope so largely developed, I am certain you will be back some day, as little Tom says, 'for good.' Barbara sends her love, and says you must write to her next. Mother says she cannot send hers, it will make the letter too heavy, after mine is in.

"Do excuse this letter; you know of old that I do not inherit any genius for writing. Do let us hear from you soon, and write everything that happens.

"I remain your loving
"Nora."

Helen read the precious letter many times that evening and for days after. It was the first letter from Brookfield, and it seemed a connecting link binding her to the happy past. Those loving, comforting letters cheered her on many a dark day through the long winter. And regularly every Monday morning they came, "white winged messengers of hope and love." Sometimes in Barbara's grave style, but oftener in Nora's rambling, warm effusions, or Mrs. Neville's kind, motherly words with their wise counsel. For, although so far away, Helen still went for advice to Mrs. Neville. Blessed are such Christian women! Verily they shall not lose their reward.

XXIII.

HAPPY DAYS.

"To sojourn in the world, and yet apart;
    To dwell with God, yet still with man to feel;
  To bear about forever in the heart
    The gladness which his Spirit doth reveal."

TWO years had passed over Helen's head; two years of quiet duty. She worked and sang and sewed and wrote letters, and one day passed much like another. She had spent the time in no vain repinings, but in contented submission to God's will; and bright, sunny spots had checkered her shady path. Brightest of these was Mr. Nelson's first visit, about a year after she left Oakdale. Helen was very glad to see him, but that joy was swallowed up in the still greater one of hearing him say,

"Helen, my daughter, we have one faith, one hope now. I too have found your Saviour."

Helen's heart overflowed in that hour with

gratitude to the all merciful Father. She scarcely
heeded the following words,

"And I owe it all to you. Had you faltered
or wavered, had you yielded to my persuasions,
and left your duty unfulfilled, all my old prejudices and skepticisms, which were beginning to
waver, would have regained their former force.
But you stood firm, my daughter, thanks be to
God; and who could help believing in a religion
which gave such steady principle to one so young?
I determined to doubt no longer. The old house
seemed desolate without you; but it was best so.
Had you still remained, I might never have
listened to the strivings of the Holy Spirit, nor
gone to Jesus for forgiveness."

After this first visit, Mr. Nelson had come often
to New York; and Helen had learned to expect him.

But the proverb says, "it is a long lane which
has no turning," and on this particular morning, everything in the house seemed turned upside down. Helen, with her head tied up, was
industriously sweeping; but notwithstanding this
busy occupation, snatches of song were constantly
bursting from her lips; and those lips that morning could certainly do nothing but smile. A rest-

27 *

less joyousness seemed to pervade her whole being; if she only moved a chair, she did it with an extra flourish of glee. Altogether work seemed more like play than labor. At length the room was finished to her satisfaction; and running out into the yard, she gathered all the flowers her garden contained, which made quite a respectable bouquet; these she put into a tumbler on the mantelpiece. Helen looked around her with pleasure; everything was clean, and as tasteful as it could be made. The room appeared just as it had before excepting that new white curtains had been hung at the windows, which gave it a light, airy appearance. The back shutters were open, and through the muslin curtains, parted and tied back with ribbon, could be seen a morning-glory which Helen had taught to climb over the window; and this she always looked at, to remind her of the country. She refused to look beyond, at the little brick yard, bounded by its board fence, but let her eye always stop at the pretty trailing vine of bright green.

Now glancing at the clock, she ran hastily up stairs, and soon returned, dressed in one of her favorite white muslins, which she had scarcely

worn since she left Oakdale. Then carefully pin-
ning up her sleeves, and skirt, and putting on an
apron, she began to get dinner. Here there was a
decided improvement; new dishes and silver
spoons. Then too, the savory roast, the variety
of vegetables and the desserts did not look much
like the meal that ordinarily graced the table of
Malcom MacGregor.

Helen had everything ready just as a carriage
drove up to the door, and Malcom and his bride
alighted. She welcomed them warmly; and
chided herself for not liking the face of her
brother's wife. But then, she could not help
thinking of what Malcom had told her a few
months before, "she was quite rich, and that was
all he cared for." Helen had talked and argued in
vain; Malcom was determined to be rich at any
cost, even, as Helen feared, at the expense of his
happiness. In one particular only, as far as she
knew, did they agree; Malcom's wife was as par-
simonious as himself. It was she who had proposed living in the same house, and foregoing
much extra expense that they might save more.

But the home-coming of a pair so uncongenial
certainly did not give that light to Helen Mac-

Gregor's eye, nor that flush of joy to her cheek. Ah, no; sad indeed would have been her lot, if forced to live in that house, whose inmates were destined to a life of discord. Her brother's marriage had released her. He had told her he would need her no longer, and Helen forgot the ingratitude of the remark in the joy of her new freedom. She wrote at once to Mrs. Neville, asking for her old place in the cottage for a short time, until she could get a school. She received an answer in the person of Mr. Nelson, indignant at the idea. Oakdale, he declared, was and always should be her home. And if she would not submit, he would use his parental authority. That afternoon she was going to Brookfield. No wonder then she felt as if she were treading on air.

The dinner dishes were all put away, and Helen had just come down stairs, in her travelling dress and bonnet, when the carriage drove up to the door and Mr. Nelson arrived. Her trunk was carried out, the short farewells were said, and Helen had left behind her the gloomy house which would long miss her cheery presence.

After that Helen seldom saw Malcom or his wife. They refused to visit Oakdale; and when

Helen stopped there for a day or two, once, when she was in New York, her brother's wife made her feel that she was not welcome. But Malcom received her very kindly; and Helen's heart yearned over her brother, who, she saw too plainly, had wrecked his happiness in this world, and refused the only consolation left him, the hope of a better life hereafter. Yes, scarcely a day passed, but Malcom became more and more conscious of the treasure he had lost in Helen. But he had his wish; he became rich; and he lived bitterly to confess that riches are powerless to confer happiness.

Steam cars travel fast, but that afternoon they could not travel fast enough for Helen's eager wishes. When they reached the depot, Mr. Nelson's carriage was waiting for them. Helen shook hands with Thomas, and almost felt like kissing the well remembered grey horses. As they drove through Brookfield, her eyes were filled with tears of thankful joy; every dear remembered spot brought back its tender recollections.

There was the little wood, in which she had been so happy and so sad. There was Lucy's poor cottage, and Mrs. Rellim's handsome house. But

v

there, hid amidst the trees and vines, was Mrs.
Neville's cottage; and yes, surely it was, Barbara
and Nora waiting at the gate. The carriage
stopped; and Helen was clasped in so many loving
arms, she was fairly carried into the house. Nora
was almost beside herself with joy. She and
Helen ran all over the house. Helen sat down in
her old place in the study, and threw herself on
her own little bed, just to try it once more, she
said laughing. Nora lay down beside her, and
throwing her arms around her exclaimed,

"Oh, Helen, I wish we could keep you here.
I have missed you so much."

"Not more than I have you, Nora darling,"
said Helen, returning the embrace, "and remember, we must make some plan to see each other
daily, since we have no little school now."

"I wish we had, so that we would be sure to
meet; for it will not be so easy for me to go out
now; since Barbara has commenced to teach I
have a great deal more to do."

"And how does Lucy like her new home?"
asked Helen.

"Very much. She sews all day, and secures a
home for herself and little Will, the baby, as we

used to call him; but he deserves the name no longer. Then besides, she earns some money. I forget how much."

"We must go down now," said Helen suddenly, getting up, "they will think us very selfish."

"Let me tell you, Helen dear, before you go down," said Nora, in a low tone, "how much I sympathized in your deep joy, when your adopted father found the dear Saviour. I could not write it."

Helen's only answer was a fond embrace, as the tears stood in her eyes.

"And Mary Rellim?" she asked, as they went down stairs, "where is she?"

"Oh, she is home now; she has finished her education. We were talking about you last evening, and planning over what nice times we will all have together next winter, if nothing happens."

When they went down they found supper ready and Mr. Nelson patiently waiting. But all inducements could not prevail on Mr. Nelson to stay to supper, as their own supper would be waiting at home; and Helen, only taking a few strawberries, because Nora said she had picked them out of her own garden for her, jumped into the carriage once more, promising to come round early the next morning.

The sun was just setting as the carriage rolled into Oakdale, and never had it looked more lovely. The warm, red light gave a mellow tint to the house; and the tall trees bent over in stately magnificence, as if guarding the spot. Flowers bloomed on every side; and Helen's head bowed in gratitude to God for a home so beautiful; and an earnest prayer went up that she might never be led astray by worldly amusements.

The servants were collected to welcome back the young girl whom they had all liked, and who was now to take her place as the head of the household. Susie was there, with her pretty face and dainty ways, and strove to show the others that she had the best right to Miss Helen.

Helen looked around her own room, and thought it was lovelier than ever, from contrast with the dingy little attic she had slept in last. She threw open the window and enjoyed the broad, beautiful landscape, and smiled to think how much more of the sky she could see here, than in her city home. Then dismissing Susie, she knelt down to give thanks for her safe return and for all God's manifold blessings.

That was a happy evening; old times seemed to live once more. Helen returned to the long neglected harp, and memories of "Auld Lang Syne" moistened her eyes, as the familiar songs woke the quiet air. They had the same old evenings,—no, not the same; for now Mr. Nelson read in the Bible, and Helen listened; and for the first time she heard him lead in prayer at family worship. All the servants were gathered together, and as a united family the petitions went up to the throne of grace.

That had been Mr. Nelson's greatest trial. Known so long to his own servants, as well as to the world, as a sneering unbeliever, how could he summon them to a religious service which he should conduct. But God giveth strength. Some of the old servants, who were Christians, rejoiced at the change, and welcomed that first effort with thankfulness. But some sneered and laughed, until they found there was a reality in their master's religion.

28

XXIV.

CONCLUSION.

> " 'Tis the quiet hour of feeling,
> Now the busy day is past,
> And tho twilight shadows stealing,
> O'er the world their mantle cast."

THE twilight of a March day was casting its lengthening shadows over life's busy hours, and calling on each weary one to hasten home to the genial fireside. The curtains were not yet drawn in the cottage parlor, but the mellow tints of coming eve mingled with the cheerful fire-light.

Mrs. Neville was in the kitchen preparing supper, and Helen, Barbara and Nora, were gathered around the fire. Silence had settled on the little group as the shadows deepened, and each one seemed lost in thought. At length Helen, putting her arm around Nora, said playfully,

" And what has become of Nora's merry tongue this evening?"

326

"Ah," said Nora with a little laugh, "I was disobeying you and thinking of next month."

"Well, I dare say we were all thinking of the same thing," said Barbara, "I cannot realize, Helen, that next month you start for Scotland."

"Scotland! Dear Scotland, shall I indeed tread your loved shore once more, and climb again your beautiful Highlands? I shall once again be a Scotch lassie and forget that years have rolled by since I hunted the heath flower, or listened for the fairies' footsteps."

"Ah, but you will be glad to come back, dear sister, will you not?" asked Nora with a little jealousy.

"Yes, very glad, I think. Here I leave warm, true hearts. Here I found a home, a father, a mother, and two dear sisters; and best of all, here I found a Saviour, and a life eternal. There none will know me; I shall return to my childhood's home, but it will be desolate, or worse still, perhaps, trodden by a stranger's foot. Yes, I shall be glad to go, but glad, very glad to come back."

We will not follow Mr. Nelson and Helen to Scotland, nor mingle in the joy of their return.

Here we bid farewell to the cottage and its inmates; to the stately halls of Oakdale, its grave master and happy young mistress. Twilight is gathering over the scene, and night will soon hide them from our view. After cares and trials await them all, but we leave them now, happy and contented; knowing well that they are treading the narrow path; that on each brow is set the Saviour's signet; and that no matter what may happen, they believe the divine words,

"Him that overcometh will I make a pillar in the temple of my God, and he shall go no more out."

THE END.

www.ingramcontent.com/pod-product-compliance
Lightning Source LLC
Chambersburg PA
CBHW031338070726
47496CB00017B/1200